Every Story a GEM!

THE RUBY FILES

AIRSHIP 27 PRODUCTIONS

The Ruby Files Vol. 1
An Airship 27 Production

"Wounds" © 2012 Andrew Salmon
"The Case of the Wayward Brother" © 2012 Bobby Nash
"Tulsa Blackie's Last Dive" © 2012 William Patrick Maynard
"Die Giftige Lilie" © 2012 Sean Taylor

Interior Illustrations © 2012 Rob Moran
Cover Illustration and Logo Design © 2012 Mark Wheatley

Editor: Ron Fortier
Associate Editor: John Bruening
Production and design by Rob Davis.

Published by Airship 27 Productions
airship27hangar.com
airship27.com

ISBN-13:978-0615609232
ISBN-10:0615609236

Printed in the United States of America

10 9 8 7 6 5 4 3 2 1

THE **RUBY FILES**
Volume One

TABLE OF CONTENTS

WOUNDS

By Andrew Salmon

The grey pall of early twilight muffled the city's raging at the gradual dying of the light. Thick pewter clouds spanned the horizon, giving the sky the appearance of an inverted bed of coals as they were touched, here and there, with the last rays of the setting December sun between the New York skyscrapers. Such skies always reminded Rick Ruby of his father and the cancerous death dreams die.

His old man had told him once, while on leave before shipping out forever twenty years ago, that overcast skies were a reminder to us down here on earth that sometimes evil is in the air, brewing hate in a cauldron as broad as the human heart, and how easy it was to forget that when the sun was shining and the sky was so blue you felt moved to tears.

However the reasons for Ruby's mood ran deeper than that. The Christmas season always brought him back to how his father had spent his last Christmas Eve: in a stinking trench in France. That evening, December 24th, 1917, the enemy overran the position and one son of a bitch had buried a bayonet in his father's chest before the attack was beaten back. His father's platoon was on the fringe of the battle and was cut off. So his father had lain there, leaking life through a pierced lung while carols were sung and the two armies crossed no man's land to show family photos, share wine and easy talk until dawn when stretcher bearers finally reached the muddy hole and carted his father off to die at the aid station.

Christmas was a time of hate for Rick Ruby. Hate for the enemy bastard who had murdered his father and hate for cruel fate that had put his dad in that position in the first place. It was irrational, he knew, but years growing up in a foster home, without a real family, skewed things a certain way and Ruby's hate was the only thing that was truly his.

Three double whiskies glowed like hot coals in Ruby's gut, stoking his ire as he strode along between the knee-high snowdrifts frosting the streets. He missed the light at the intersection and passed the seconds thinking of the old man, heavy skies and the isolation of the deserted street corner.

The distant tinkle of broken glass made him turn his gaze slightly to an alley across the street. On the third floor fire escape between two blocky tenements rubbing shoulders, he saw fractions of shadowed figures engaged in what appeared to be a tug of war. One side worked from inside an open window, obscured by billowing curtains and the closeness of the neighboring building, the other fought for purchase on the slick, grilled metal floor of the fire escape landing. The light changed, but Ruby stood transfixed. The guy on the landing—it was a guy he could see now, although the alley was draped in shadow—was losing the battle and was being hauled through the window.

Ruby's first thought was that this was none of his business—that he was tired after playing peeper all afternoon on an infidelity case and just wanted to shut up the office and call it a night. Crimes were being committed all over the city and ten thousand cops couldn't stop them all. A brief stint on the force left no doubt in his mind on that score. He was a civilian and had learned to live with it long ago. His P.I. license did not have spaces for gold stars for duty above and beyond the call and, frankly, he plain wasn't in the mood.

The light was red again and Ruby still hadn't moved. The man being devoured by the window had been reduced to frantically kicking legs swathed in twisted, bunched blue trousers and ended in broken down, flailing shoes. The blue reminded him of that life he'd put behind him. Worn, smooth soles completed the memory.

The man being dragged inside was a cop.

Ruby darted glances this way and that for a harness bull to pass this off to. He was alone on the avenue. The traffic light in front of him burned with green flame.

Cursing, a plume of breath curling up into the frosty air, Ruby shuffled across the street. The breeze through the intersection fanned the flames of his unruly head of red hair and he regretted not wearing a hat. He lost sight of the struggle coming across as the angle changed. By the time he stood outside the alley the man had vanished. Ruby looked up at the landing and saw only slivers of sky through the steel rods. He let some long minutes tick by.

A muffled scream lanced down at him where he stood with his feet embedded in old, crumbled newspapers jutting out of the snow. Compelled to act, he cursed again as he leaped upwards, his tall, muscular frame defying gravity for a second until hard hands grasped the cold, rusted bottom rung of the ladder the combatants had pulled up after them. He had to catch the ladder when he touched down for fear of giving away his presence below the third storey window. He grunted as gravity toyed with the heavy bar in his fists, but he was able to gently lower it to the cracked, frozen asphalt.

The silence of the window with the billowing ivory curtains gave him a thousand nightmares to consider on the way up. There had just been the one terrible cry and then silence. The curtains snapped and curled above him.

He reached the landing, crouched low beneath the sill and held his breath lest the steam rise up past the open window to give him away to anyone watching inside. The curtains sounded like the surf now as they scraped along the rough brick. A faint burning smell reached him where he pressed against the wall. Someone had left a pot on the stove. With the smell of char came a low moan from inside the room – garbled, unintelligible.

Ruby yanked his piece, got rid of the safety and placed the ends of the fingers of his free hand on the lip of the sill. Gun poised, he inched his head up to peer into the room. Any cop would tell you he'd prefer a run and gun shootout to framing himself in a doorway or window of a strange room, but there was nothing for it. Inch by agonizing inch, his gaze moved up the chipped red brick to the tombstone grey of the jutting sill while too many bad memories of the potential horrors awaiting him inside the room tugged at his concentration.

His gaze crested the sill and his eyes bugged at the insanely laughing clown's face staring across the sill at him. Ruby's breath exploded out of him. He cried out and reeled back. Vertigo drove into his gut as his spine pushed against the slats of the icy railing and he teetered on the brink, his shoes skating along the steel.

Flailing, he seized the sill with his free hand, the fingers all but thrust into the gaping maw of the clown braying silent laughter and transfixing him with sightless, lifeless wide eyes.

The clown head floated in the window, bodiless. Its expression fixed as though carved in stone. As reason returned to Ruby he saw the clown for what it was: a decal stuck on the worn, off-center drawer of a child's high bureau someone had pushed up against the window. Ruby steadied his breathing and chewed on that. If the attackers who had abducted the cop wanted to block any possible escape, then why hadn't they simply locked the window?

The whimpering moan drifted out to Ruby again.

Courage restored although his heart still hammered in his chest, Ruby moved with fragile confidence. Convinced no enemy awaited him since his clanging and flopping around like a fish on the metal grill had drawn no interest from whoever was in the room, he stood framed in the window now and peered past the tall dresser which had been decorated with tiny, peeling, faded decals of horses, cowboys, spacemen and masked vigilantes to go with the large clown face.

He could hear the moan clearly now. It was coming from the left but the room was dim. The burning smell reached him with pungent intensity. The cooking pot was inside somewhere.

When the moan came a third time, Ruby let his eyes follow the sound and saw the back of a man's head poking up half blocked by an arm chair at an angle to the window. He could not see the man's face, but discerned that he was sitting on the floor, his back against the front of the chair. Ruby's eyes adjusted with agonized slowness and he made out a blue shoulder.

He'd found the cop.

Every sense alert, he threw glances around the darkened room. The sun chose that moment to break through the clouds and blazed across the battered face of the dresser dazzling his strained eyes. It was as if a star spangled curtain had dropped across the window.

Throwing caution to the wind, Ruby pushed against the dresser but it held fast as though bolted to the floor. They must have piled furniture up against it to barricade the window. The burning smell intensified and he thought he saw a cloud of black smoke roiling down the narrow corridor beyond the sprawled cop.

"Can you move?" he shouted at the prone officer.

The man's head twitched and then bobbed as if he was still struggling to escape his tormentors.

"They're gone!" Ruby assured. "Look! There's something burning in there and I can't get in. If the door's not an option, get over here, crawl if you have to, and maybe we can squeeze you through."

The head bowed and, for a moment, Ruby thought the man was dead. He saw the sodden brown hair, the matted uniform. Whatever they had done to the cop he was sweating buckets from it now. Ruby called out again but the man's attention seemed focused on something in his lap or between his legs.

Ruby hissed when a hand as red as the devil's came into view near the man's head. The palsied fingers dripped blood. The hand fell and came up again with something pink and shiny held with trembling tenderness. Realization brought bile to Ruby's throat and he gagged.

"Christ! They gutted him." Ruby recoiled, then hawked and spat. He braced his back against the far railing and was about to try to kick his way in when he realized the implication of what he had just seen. The man was trying to stuff his guts back into his body. Even if Ruby got in, moving the sap would kill him for sure. Flames now danced with the smoke coming up the corridor, drawn by the cross breeze through the window. Ruby could close the window and prolong the man's agony as the flames ate their way towards him or he could leave it open and speed the guy on the way to oblivion.

"Patrolman! What's your name? Who did this to you?"

Ruby pressed his cheeks into the crevice between the window frame and the dresser. The man moaned and then began whispering gibberish. It took a moment for Ruby to realize the guy was speaking in a foreign language. The close proximity of death had robbed the dying man of his English. Flames crackled a few feet from the man.

Ruby kicked out the window in the hopes of clearing a space to crawl through. He opened his mouth to shout again, but another odor reached him with that of the thick black smoke.

"Shit!"

Ruby dropped below the sill just as the room exploded. Flames stabbed out with a roaring whoosh, setting the curtains ablaze. The moans inside turned to high-pitched screams as the kerosene the man had been doused with ignited. It was this odor Ruby had caught a split-second before the explosion.

The fire began devouring the building. Ruby was sitting atop a powder keg. Doors banged inside, shouts rang and feet trampled along wooden floors. Ruby took the hint and, crouching beneath the licking flames, made it to the ladder and started down. The gun in his right hand slowed his progress and he had to pause on the first landing to holster the weapon.

Sirens wailed in the distance, drawing closer. Ruby reached the end of the ladder and dropped down to the cold alley and stared up at the iron sky between the rails once more. Tenants began thrusting legs out windows to reach the fire escape while others were already clear, crowding around the front of the building. Ruby joined them to wait for the police to arrive and claim what was left of their own.

※ ※ ※

One of the two prowl cars to arrive on the scene was a radio unit and Ruby extricated himself from the staring throng hypnotized by the pyre comprised of their earthly goods and shuffled over to have the unit put a call in to Jack McGinnis who pulled up in an unmarked sedan ten minutes later. Ruby shoved away the hand of a paramedic trying to tie an oxygen mask over the lower half of his face and strode over.

He lit a cigarette, drew deeply while sidestepping a cluster of firefighters running hoses out of fire plugs slowly transforming into ice sculptures and came up alongside the detective's vehicle.

"What's the spill?" Detective McGinnis demanded. He was alone in the car.

"Where's that fool partner of yours?"

"I left him with Mason down at the 87th coaxing witnesses to eyeball a suspect in a robbery-homicide. The scumbags are pulling heists dressed as ghosts these days. It's playing hell with getting a positive ID. Don't keep me waiting, Rick."

Ruby's expression darkened. "Before the place went up a blue suit got hauled in there. They cut him up, Mac, left him to burn."

McGinnis ran a hard hand through his dark hair, then rammed the door handle and climbed out to stare at the flaming ruin. He jammed his hands into the pockets of his grey overcoat swathing his medium build. "You recognize him?"

"I quit the force a long time ago."

"Did you know him!"

"Dunno, Mac," Ruby replied, rubbing at his nose. "All I saw were his legs and the back of his head when I tried to reach him." Ruby relayed the scene to McGinnis who listened with slitted eyes.

"All right." McGinnis got on the squawk box and put a call in. He cradled the handset and turned to Ruby. "It's end of watch. We'll see who hasn't made it back."

"You say you tried to get at him and couldn't get a name or face?"

"Like I said, his back was turned and he was babbling in a language I never heard."

"That's something," McGinnis said. The radio crackled and the detective leaned in through the open window to take the call. "Four of us are in Emergency," he relayed to Ruby. "A cracked ankle chasing a pincher, swan dive down a flight of steps after a second storey man, two dribbled their heads against the dash in a fender-bender. Only one unaccounted for in this neighborhood is Peter Dacso. Speaking a weird lingo, you said? Figures. Dacso's a bozgor."

"Hungarian, huh?" Ruby considered. "That's as good a bet as any, I suppose. I couldn't make sense of his jabbering."

"I'll take a wild guess he was begging for help or telling you who cut him."

"Yeah."

They stood in awkward silence for a minute. McGinnis pulled his hands out of his pockets and looked over the roof of his car at the spraying fire plug across the street. Snow tumbled off the awning of the butcher shop over there and splashed in the partially hardened skating rink forming up around the hydrant. "Say, Rick, thanks for calling this in and sticking around to dot 'i's', I mean that. Come in sometime over the next couple of days and swear out a statement. What happened here is over. It's in the coroner's hands. You can saddle up and ride."

"Reporters are already snooping around. Cannock from the Gazette was scoping me before you pulled up. So what's with the brush off?"

"I saw him. The blue suits will keep the reporters back until I say so." McGinnis sighed and fixed his brown eyes on Rick's. "You don't carry a shield anymore. That leaves you out of certain things. You know how it works."

"Yeah, I know all about it."

"Don't be like that. The door swings both ways."

"Just before it smacks you in the teeth."

McGinnis glanced around conspiratorially, then leaned in to rasp at Ruby. "Word has it Peter Dacso wasn't all right. That's all I'm saying."

"Another crooked cop, Mac? I'm shocked."

"Everyone who puts on the uniform gets a little dirty," McGinnis said.

"I know it. That's one reason I traded mine for a license."

McGinnis got hot. "Don't give me that. Tell me you got by without skimming a little and I'll call you a liar. It don't matter if you accept a free sandwich at the lunch counter when you could pay your freight at the Automat, take cop rates at the laundry or a plate of homemade biscuits for the missus from the old lady next door. It's offered to make sure we keep a firm grip on the leash of the wolf howling at their front doors. That's all right as far as it goes. So long as a little is a lot. But when a cop gets big, hungry eyes, that's when it starts to spiral down the crapper. You've got some tarnish yourself, friend. Pretty sweet deal they cut you on the rent over at Belle's in exchange for services rendered. You pay for all that booze you bathe in down in the taproom?"

"I'm going home," Ruby said.

McGinnis nodded, satisfied. "Be seeing you."

Ruby stopped by the office first in the hopes of catching Edie, his secretary, before she left for the day. All he found was a note on his desk telling him two payments had come in and she was stopping by the bank on her way home. He locked up the office and made for the bedroom.

A squirming dance under the cold jet of the shower washed the stink of stale sweat, soot and fear off him as he tried his best to forget the sight of Dacso sitting there, kicking in his own gore while the flames ate their way towards him. But it was immediately clear to him that it was going to have to be a liquid cure, taken internally, for what ailed him. He dressed and headed over to the Boom Boom Club to fill the prescription.

The trip wasn't just about a balm for his ills, Ruby reminded himself. When a cop goes down in the line the way Dacso did, you weren't looking at some crazed hophead or street punk to tumble for it. Killings like Dacso usually had backing and Ruby wanted to know who was behind it so he'd know which way to jump should it come to that. For that kind of information, the Boom Boom was the place to be. Also, the joint was a show bar and, brother, did they put on a show.

Ruby arrived a few minutes before the floor show began and was at his usual table sipping straight up scotch when things kicked into high gear.

The lights dimmed and the drummer did a barrel roll on the tom-toms. Donna Dixon, the star attraction, hit the stage with more fanfare than the President garners and a lusty cheer roared up. Dixon was wearing the wispy memory of a form-fitting evening gown that conformed to every plane of her tall cool form. Platinum blonde hair cascaded down over one eye, leaving the other ice blue oval to raise the temperature in the room to the boiling point. Bombastic music erupted from the band and Dixon set about turning that memory of a dress into a distant memory. The music reached its crescendo as did most of the male customers.

When the house lights came up, Ruby was already backstage. He was known to the bouncers who paid him no mind. He rapped on Donna Dixon's door.

"It's open, Rick," a velvety smooth voice purred from the other side.

Dixon was draped in a pink, terry cloth bathrobe and slouched on a frilly couch, her bare legs crossed at the ankles, one arm bent at the elbow perched on the arm of the sofa, a cigarette in the long-fingered hand.

"Hey, baby," Rick said and his smile stretched from ear to ear.

"Hi yourself." Dixon pouted. "I saw you out there. Sober as a judge. This isn't a social call so what do you want?"

"Is that any way to talk?"

"It is when this girl hasn't seen hide nor hair of you in the last week. Been playing doctor with that secretary of yours, I bet!"

"Work, baby. Work," Ruby said as he lit a cigarette. "You know how it is."

"I know all right. Well, this gal has to work again in about thirty minutes and needs her beauty rest. So I'll say it again, what do you want?"

Ruby would have liked to have shown Dixon just how glad he was to see her but with things off kilter he couldn't completely forget his troubles even for a dish like the vision before him. And there was information he simply had to have. Dixon used her position at the club to pick up mob talk she passed on to the police, and Ruby, for a fee. Things were tough all over and unattached burlesque dancers had to pay the rent, too.

"I'll lay it out for you," Ruby said with great reluctance. "What are you hearing about that tenement fire?"

Dixon yanked her legs off the table and sat up, allowing the robe to fall open to give Ruby a sample of what he was most likely going to be missing for a long while. "Where that cop got it? It was in the special editions." Ruby nodded and Dixon went on. "All I know is what I read." Concern for Ruby put a dainty crease between her captivating eyes. "But I will tell you this: someone is trying to muscle in on Shairp's action. Word is there's competition crawling in from the docks. Some say Shairp's territory is ripe for the picking. It's all his goons worry about these days when they give up trying to paw me. You watch yourself, Rick. Now blow!"

Ruby thanked her and put a ten on the dresser. Cursing under his breath at having to make such a hasty departure, Ruby came around the stage and headed for the door. He turned what Dixon had told him over in his thoughts. Anyone who knew the streets knew that the syndicate controlling a neighborhood leaned on their rented cops when a gang war was about to erupt. Muscle and intimidation only came after the first shots were fired. However corrupt officers were not averse to working both sides of the street as they didn't care where their dirty money came from. McGinnis had intimated to Ruby that the dead cop was in it up to his neck. That tracked. The fact that the streets weren't already running red with blood meant that the dirty cops were still taking bids. Either that or the fuse was lit and the streets were about to explode. Either way, Ruby took

Dixon's warning to heart. Whatever was about to break, he didn't want to have anything to do with it.

For the next forty-eight hours, Ruby worked the peeper case. A mailman was tomcatting around on his fat wife of eighteen years, and the wife's brother needed to get the goods on the sap so they could rake him over the coals in court. Ruby got those goods in the form of 8 X 10 Polaroids and took the brother's money while doing it. These were not actions they'd write sonnets about and no amount of showers would wash this taint off, but a guy had to make a living, and earning your daily bread from the misery of others was one way to do it.

Ruby didn't follow the Dacso investigation in the papers. Belle had showed him his name on the front page of the evening *Gazette* that first night, and that was it as far as Ruby was concerned. Cops investigating cops in the midst of a brewing gang war were blades of a meat grinder, and no private citizen—or private investigator for that matter—put themselves in the middle of that. This was what Mac and Donna had been trying to tell him, and his ears worked just fine. Thing was, the scene at the tenement was burned into Ruby's grey matter, but it could take a number as far as his nightmares went. Involving himself any more than that would be suicide, and he wasn't that far gone yet.

Until the old man showed up.

The third morning after Peter Dacso's murder, Edie Rose Adams, Rick's secretary, sidled into the office and interrupted his third black coffee. She was medium height with a slick mane of chestnut brown, chin-length hair, a strong graceful jaw and wide-set, deep brown eyes. Her full lips sneered lovingly at the hangover symptoms Ruby displayed.

"There's a character out there looking to see you, Rick," she announced in her voice tinged with a throaty rasp.

"He look like money?"

"More than spare change, less than a c-note."

"Pretty big gap these days," Ruby observed, his watery eyes fixed on the pool of black coffee in front of his dry lips. "Be more specific."

"You're the boss," Adams sneered. "He's about sixty but looks ten years older. Got a nice face that's had more life than most shoved into it and has got the scars to prove it." She paused. "His name's Alexei Dacso, the father of the dead cop."

Ruby blinked. "Tell him I'm busy."

"Don't be like that, Rick. He told me he saw your name in the paper the other day and that you're the only one can help him. He's interested in the truth."

"Then take him to the mission with you the next time you run out there on your errands of mercy. I'm busy."

Adams, seeing she wouldn't get any farther with Ruby, turned smartly on her sensible heels and stormed out, much to Ruby's satisfaction. At the sound of the name he'd heard those grinder blades start up in his head, and knew he needed to pull the plug before they really started to whir. Questions about the Dacso killing had already taken root in his brain matter. The last thing they needed was fertilizer. Dacso Sr. could go to the cops if he wanted to know what had happened to his boy. He kept telling himself that all morning until he went out into the snow on the fraud case for an insurance company.

Alexei Dacso was a vague memory when Ruby planted himself on his usual stool where the bar at Belle's made a right turn and ordered the first drink of the evening. He raised the shot of rye up to his lips and his eyes met those of an old man perched at the opposite end. The haggard face was carved from stone but the red-rimmed blue eyes blazed in the pale skull, the gaze fixed right on him. He didn't need a sign around the old man's neck to know it was Alexei Dacso.

Ruby finished his drink and calmly put the glass down. It was a free country, and if Dacso wanted to keep a barstool warm he was welcome to it. Ruby was thinking differently four hours later when the old man was still staring at him along the length of the bar. Like a mannequin, the old fool just sat and stared, waiting, daring Ruby to make the next move.

He did. He went upstairs to his room.

But the old man was there the next night and the one after that. Always on the same stool, the eyes as unblinking as a vulture's, fixed on Ruby as the private investigator tried to wash away another sordid day. The old man watched and waited. It crawled beneath Ruby's skin. Who the hell was this old fool to stare at him like he'd drowned a sack of kittens? His son's death was the cops' problem, not his. Ex-cops got into the P.I. racket to be their own bosses, and with that came leave to refuse any damn client they didn't want. Ruby began to squirm under the stare. He turned to face the rows of bottles but caught Dacso's face reflected in the mirror behind the bar. Turning the other way drew the eyes of hookers and husband hunters with more problems than he was willing to deal with at the moment.

Finally, ten minutes before closing time on the third night, Ruby slid off his stool and strode unsteadily over to the old man.

"Ain't you got any place to go?" Ruby demanded. Three days of being staring at had put a sour taste in his gut.

"I ain't got no one no more," Dacso replied, his eyes still trained on Ruby's vacated stool.

Ruby sighed and shook his head. "You win, pops," he hissed. "I'll give you five minutes."

Dacso took his time turning his gaze up to meet Ruby's. There was no reaction in the placid, drooping features. He did not speak. Instead he shoved his unfinished beer to one side, scooped up his change, left a nickel, and came down off the stool.

He stood before Ruby, his hat in his hand. "My name is Alexei Dacso."

"I know who you are."

Dacso placed his hat on his head. "You are tired, Mr. Ruby," he said in a chalky, accented voice. "We will talk tomorrow. Noon." He rattled off the address of a diner on 7th, then turned and walked out of the bar into the raging blizzard howling outside the fogged door.

※ ※ ※

The Gunga Diner was at the corner of 40th and 7th, but Ruby didn't need the address to find the place. The store front gleamed black and there was a neon sign out front had a big pink and purple elephant with a howdah on it that stuck out like a sore thumb. Dacso was seated at a round window like a giant porthole on the right as Ruby came in. He could barely make the old man out as the place was an Indian joint and waves of spice and curry laden steam made his eyes water and misted the mirror covering one wall.

Ruby grunted at Dacso, shook the snow off his jacket and took a seat. The sooner this was over with, the better.

Dacso sensed Ruby's discomfort. "Please forgive my choice of meeting place. I developed a taste for Indian food when I lived in that country after the Great War."

"I ate already. Don't worry about it."

"My father fought in the war between the states," Dacso rambled, "his

"Please forgive my choice of meeting place."

left arm fertilizes the soil around Sutherland Station in Virginia. Tired and disillusioned, he returned to Hungary with my mother who carried me inside. So, you see, we are two Americans, yes? It was my father's wish that I return here one day. When my Anna died in childbirth, I honoured that wish and came here with my son, Peter, to open a delicatessen."

"I ain't got all day, old timer," Ruby interrupted. "Why are you telling me this?"

"Because I wish you to see that my grandfather loved this country, that I love this country, that I believe in democracy and wanted my Peter to grow up an American. I filled his head with these dreams and he joined the police force to protect these ideas. Peter was a good boy."

"Prisons, graveyards and battlefields are filled with good boys, Dacso. Look, put the flag away and tell me what you want!"

A waiter in a sari took Dacso's order. Ruby called for coffee.

"Find my son's killers."

"You're talking foolish, old man. The police are all over it. When one of their own goes down, they beat the bushes. You've lived here long enough to know that. There's nothing I can do for you."

"But they only go through motions. Three days and they tell me nothing!"

"Investigations take time," Ruby offered, blandly.

"Do not give me the hogwash!" Dacso's accent was pushing through with his emotions. "What you do in their place?"

"I don't know. Rustle up witnesses, find out who rented the room they left him in."

"Ya! They have not done. See what I tell you!"

Ruby had to admit that this was queer. However the old man didn't know what he was asking. If Dacso was as crooked as Mac seemed to think, the dead man would have rough friends on the force looking to cover their tracks and protect their interests. Every dirty cop knows the stakes they play for once they start down this twisting path and will do anything to keep their neck out of the noose. They wouldn't bat an eye at tossing a P.I. down the rabbit hole.

"Money I have. I pay."

"It's not a question of money, Dacso."

"Then, what?"

"I can't help you. I wish I could, but I can't."

Ruby tossed a nickel down on the table and got up. Dacso's withered, sinewed hand gripped his forearm, tugging intently.

"Nothing have I now!" he hissed. "They take my world from me, tell me it was rotten to begin with. I will not stand for that!"

Ruby took his seat and leaned in until their faces were mere inches apart. "I'll spell it out for you! Your boy got mixed up in a black cesspool of corruption and went under. I've splashed around in that pool when my girl was cut to ribbons by the type of men your son was involved with. Christ! It's been almost ten years!" He blinked then his gaze bore into Dacso's. "I put away the guy I was sure did it and he bought his way out. He's walking around free as a bird. That's how this will end. You and me will both wind up dead along with your boy and the guilty will be free to drag the world into the gutter. Is this how you want your last days to go?"

Dacso hung his head and two tears glinted down his unshaven cheeks. Ruby leaned back and stared out at the world outside the window with a sneer. He hadn't wanted to be so hard on the old guy but what choice had Dacso left him?

"Are you a father?" Dacso asked feebly.

"I told you they punched my girl full of holes," Ruby spat, still staring out at the street.

"And your father? You see him? You are close?"

"My father died back in '17. Killed in action."

Dacso glanced past Ruby and read the headline declaring Hitler's threats on the paper a guy was reading at the next table. "We stand on the brink of war again! Terrible!" Then his eyes swung back to Ruby. "The loss of your father, it is with you always, yes?"

Ruby thought back to the years he spent in the foster home after his old man didn't make it back and that familiar bitterness burned in his gut. He'd wasted years hating the enemy that had taken his father from him, imagined killing him with his bare hands at night when the stars winked mockingly outside his bedroom window and sleep was as far away as the moon. That bile had led him to join the police force—so he could prevent what happened to him from happening to others or, at least stop his share of the evil plotters who wanted the world to burn. Only it hadn't been that simple in the end. The corruption ran too deep and eventually stole the best part of him. He spent six years looking for it at the bottom of a glass and got nowhere. Now here he was with a license and a shit-hole office trying to put things right again like some punch drunk over-the-hill fighter kidding himself he still had the goods. Goddamn Dacso anyway!

"I tell you what I'll do," Ruby said at last. "I'll ask around. Quietly. If anything turns, I'll bring it to the cops. That's the best I can do."

Dacso's expression brightened. "Thank you! Thank you! You are a good man. You will need money, yes?"

"Damn right you're going to pay me!" Ruby insisted. "It'll cover the cost of my funeral."

Ruby got shed of Dacso as quickly as he could after learning from the old man that the tenants of the burned apartment house had been taken in at Keeler Mission on 21st. Dacso had not been able to find out where the building manager had got to. The old man had continued carrying on when they were back on the street and Ruby started thinking he'd grown another pair of legs. Finally free of the old fool, he decided to try the mission and called himself every kind of a fool as he hopped a tram to 20th then had to walk one block over in the blizzard.

The Keeler Mission was cut out of one wall of a red brick building connected to a baker's at the corner. A single glass-paneled door with half curtains gave on a large rectangular box of mustard yellow walls dominated by four long tables populated with the former residents of the tenement sipping soup with the odd hobo sprinkled in amongst the crowd. The room was thick with cigarette smoke, and at first glance, it looked as if the survivors of the tenement fire still smouldered from that blaze. The small potbelly stove against one wall chuffed feeble heat and the room would have been cold if not for the accumulated body heat turning the place into a sauna. A kitchen against the far wall was doling out soup to a thin line on the other side of the railing dividing the kitchen from the rest of the room. On the left, next to the telephone, was a small stage with a sagging piano. Scrawny kids ran this way and that, playing the only game they knew as they practiced shooting each other with cocked fingers or plastic cap pistols.

Ruby didn't see anyone who looked like they ran the place, but caught the flurry of movement in the kitchen through the window cut in the wall so that the victuals could be passed from the kitchen to the line up. He headed over. On the way, he was struck by the livid covers of the goofy magazines like the ones he'd seen cluttering up newsstands everywhere. Rocketships blasted off to a million strange worlds, slavering bug-eyed monsters pointed rayguns at square-jawed heroes with fishbowls on their heads.

"You noticed the decor, huh?" A man came alongside Ruby. He was a large black man with kind eyes and an easy smile. A chef's apron covered his worn jeans and work shirt. The shirt sleeves were rolled up and cabled forearms worked as the man dried his hands on a towel. The big forearms bore old knife cuts that crawled like fat fish-belly white worms. The scars and the scatter of hayseed in his baritone spoke of trials darker than any shade of night. The eyes, mild as warm milk, eyed Ruby evenly. "Everybody does. They're for the lady who started up the place after the crash. Only dreams she had were bigger than the world and she used to try to pull the bums up with talk of a bright future."

"If she's around, I'd like a word," Ruby said.

"Naw. She passed. She stepped out that front door with her beau and was run down just like that. Going on ten years now." His expression grew wistful. "The good Lord must'a had a good reason to call her home when He did." He came out of his reverie, regarded Ruby and smiled. "The current boss is out picking up donations. With the extra mouths on account of the fire what we have doesn't go far. I'm sorta unofficially in charge when Mr. Howard is away. Name's Collier."

"Rick Ruby. With your permission, Mr. Collier, I'd like to have a word with the survivors from that tenement fire."

"You the law?"

"Private."

Collier considered for a moment before saying, "I guess there's no harm in that. Just try not to upset them too much. They lost everything they had, and all they've got now comes courtesy of strangers. I'll ask you to go easy on them."

"What I need won't bother them much at all."

Collier thought about it before motioning with the towel in his hands. "Go on then."

Ruby made a circuit of the shabby room. They came in all shapes and sizes but the uniting feature was a look of lean desperation they all exhibited. There was an old lady in a tattered frock being fawned over by a group of tenants. Guessing she was a resident of long standing well known to the other tenants, Ruby elbowed his way through the group fluffing the old lady's pillows and moving her soup so it was within reach and politely asked her who had lived in the apartment on the east side of the building, third floor. The crone was a little batty and replied in a queenly manner that she did not know but that the manager might, except he wasn't at the mission. However she stabbed a gnarled, bony finger at a young couple sitting at the table closest to the door and told him that they had lived on the third floor. Ruby nodded his thanks as the old lady was apparently hard of hearing and headed over.

One look at the couple told him that they'd been around the block a few times and could give guided tours. That meant honesty was out. This pair looked out for themselves and had learned not to stick their necks out for anyone unless there was something in it for them. Ruby knew just the trick.

"Some nerve, you prick!" the woman was saying, shoving the man with her hard in the ribs. "Treating a woman in a family way like that!"

"Ah, cram it!" the man replied shoving back. "I'll break your mouth for ya, then you'll know what treatin's all about!"

The woman looked to be about five months along but there was nothing delicate about her. She'd been a looker, Ruby could see that right off even under the extra weight she'd put on during her pregnancy and he got the impression he was getting a preview of how she'd look ten years down the line. She had a mane of dark hair, a full mouth and eyebrows so thick that they should have spoiled her square face and good cheekbones. The birthmark on her cheek was pure affectation. The hunger in her eyes for all that the world had denied her was going to be Ruby's way to get to her. The guy was a little runt of a man with a mop of curly red hair offset by a natty purple pinstripe suit. Over the back of his chair was a shit-brown leather overcoat that looked like it had been used to cover a capstan down at the docks for a few years. A cruel, downturned mouth, jutting cheekbones and beady blue eyes offset the spray of freckles Nature had tossed across his nose and cheeks as a cruel joke.

"Excuse me," Ruby said, breaking in on their cursing. "My name is Ferguson. I wonder if I might have a word with you."

"Wonder someplace else," the man spat. "Can't you see we're busy?"

Ruby took the rebuke in silence because he saw the woman's eyes slide over his muscular frame as she considered trading up. It was time to sink the hook. "I'm sorry to bother you," he purred. "I represent Chemical Insurance and we're trying to track down a beneficiary for a policy that is giving us nothing but headaches."

"You look like John Law," the woman said.

"Yeah, I get that all the time," Ruby replied. "As I said, I've been assigned to track down this beneficiary – "

"That's nice," the man sneered. "I'll say it again. Shove off!"

Ruby went on. "The agency is prepared to pay a sizable reward to whoever can assist us in this matter."

"Reward?" the woman spoke her appraising eyes quit their roaming and locked on Ruby's.

"Why didn't you say so in the first place?" The man's demeanour changed in a heartbeat. "How can we help?

The woman made an attempt at being coquettish that failed miserably with the beach ball under her faded house dress. "Sylvia Kovacs, Mr. Ferguson." She offered a plump hand to Ruby who didn't know if he was expected to shake it or kiss it. "This is Charlie."

"Pleasure, Ferguson," Charlie said without meaning it.

"Nice to meet you," Ruby lied. "I'm told you fine folks lived on the third floor of the tenement that burned down. On the east side of the building second from the end?"

"Yes! That's true we did," Kovacs nodded eagerly as if they were discussing a secret treasure map and had just made a fantastic discovery that boded well for them.

"Good. Now we're getting places," Ruby said. "Do you happen to know who lived in the last apartment on that side?"

"Their name was Smith," Charlie said and brayed laughter. This was Ruby's first indication the man was half-tanked. For a small man he held his liquor well. "Pay up!"

"That's just not true, Charlie," Kovacs replied girlishly. Ruby's guts churned. "Now let's see, what was their name?"

Ruby could see the woman was deliberately dragging things out, probably with the hope of raising the stakes. He'd already had just about enough of these two. "Well, if it comes to you, I'll be around. Asking the other tenants on the floor."

"You see what you did, you brainless slut!"

"Who you calling brainless? Why if I wasn't carrying your kid, I'd leave you cold and then where would you be?"

"In Heaven, tramp! That kid ain't mine and you're going to find me gone one of these days!"

This seemed to genuinely panic the woman who dropped all pretense and gave Ruby what he wanted. He didn't like it.

"It was the Petersons, all right! They went back to Baltimore when he got laid off at the furniture plant. The place was empty ever since. Did I do okay?"

Ruby hid his disappointment well. "Ah, there we go. You've been a big help." He made a show of taking down their names and let them prattle on in case they spilled anything that might be of use to him. He had to tell them three times that he understood they'd be staying at the mission for the foreseeable future and that he could reach them there when the reward was paid out.

"And don't go sending that reward care of the manager!" Charlie cautioned. "He's as crooked as a broke dick dog!"

Finally the pair had given Ruby something to go on. He put on his phony nice act again and asked them for the manager's name so that he could red flag it in the Peterson file. Shairp. Ed Shairp.

Ruby knew the moniker. Ed Shairp was Lou Shairp's little brother. And the Shairp syndicate ran the neighbourhood rackets.

It was time for another talk with McGinnis.

❈ ❈ ❈

The cold deepened with the sunset and Ruby left a message with Dispatch for McGinnis to meet him at the Boom Boom Club. On the surface, meeting in a mob-controlled place to discuss Ruby's unwelcome poking into the Dacso killing seemed like a death wish, but the two men often met there over a beer, and the hope here was that sticking to the routine announced to anyone interested that the meet was nothing to get bent out of shape about.

McGinnis found Ruby nursing a whiskey sour at a table to the left of the wide stage against the wall.

"What gives, Rick?" McGinnis asked as he dropped into one of the padded chairs.

"I hear the department is stalling on the Dacso investigation."

McGinnis started, then relaxed as realization spread across his features. "The old man."

"Well?"

"Rick I told you to steer clear of that. What's the matter with you?"

"That's not an answer."

"It's all the answer you're entitled to," the detective hissed. "I just caught the squawk that the bodies of three ex-cons turned up in a dumpster over on Lafayette and they were part of the Sanfori group that got chased out of the docks."

"They're the ones trying to strong-arm the Shairp group?"

McGinnis was impressed by how much Ruby knew but didn't show it. "Something's started, Rick. You've got that part right. But you've got no idea what you're messing with here. Leave it alone."

"Can't do it, Mac." Rick shook his head slightly and downed the last of his drink. "The Dacso kid was killed in one of Shairp's buildings."

"We know." McGinnis put a calloused hand on Rick's forearm. "Listen to me. What I told you at the scene a few days back about the kid? It's a lot of bunk. Get me?" He leaned in casually for the sake of prying eyes but his voice betrayed the emotion behind the words. "Dacso had gone under to get the goods on officers Lou Shairp has on the payroll. He got killed for his trouble. But the investigation is still open. Captain Connors signed off on it weeks ago, but he did it quiet. He only just put me wise to it because Dacso's old man was making too much noise and word was you were involved. I copped that bit about Peter Dacso having turned a day or so before the fire and thought it was the McCoy until Connors set me straight. The kid was clean."

Ruby was surprised at how relieved he felt for Dacso Sr. as he listened to McGinnis's spiel. "This on the level?"

"What kind of talk is that?" McGinnis asked, offended. "You and me don't always see eye to eye, but I'm your friend and wouldn't lie about a thing like this. Not even to save your worthless hide. Not to mention the old man's. He's been shouting from the rooftops about his dead son and sooner rather than later his squawk is going to reach the wrong ears. Maybe it already has."

"Okay, I believe you."

"Good. Now believe this. Rooting out dirty cops unleashes two kinds of holy hell when it breaks. On the one hand there are a whole lot of lowlifes who'll be looking to cover their tracks and, on the other, a handful of officers pressed into a corner. A cop off the leash can be a dangerous animal, Rick. I'm not telling you anything you don't already know."

Rick leaned back and threw an arm over the back of his chair and grimaced. "I knew it was nuts mixing in this. What do I tell the old man?"

"Anything but the truth or he could sour the deal. Get him to call off the dogs. If not, there's no telling who might get it. If this operation comes off, a few desperate individuals on both sides of the law might slip the net and they will be looking to avenge their wounds, Rick. You and the old man steer clear, you hear?"

"I hear you, Mac. But there's something isn't right about the whole thing. Take Dacso for instance. If he knew the score, why did he let Shairp's men drag him up that fire escape? He had his whistle and his piece. He could have touched off a racket that would have sent them running."

"You're saying he went willingly."

"What it looks like."

"They might have had a gun on him. Everyone goes willingly with a barrel in the ribs. Maybe he was playing it cagey and it backfired."

"Maybe. I don't know."

McGinnis finished his drink, dropped a bill on the bar and left. Ruby hadn't liked where he'd left things with Donna Dixon, but she didn't reply to his repeated knocks on her dressing room door.

Ruby sensed walls closing in and didn't like it. McGinnis corroborated what Dixon had told him and it looked as if Ruby had really stepped in it. It didn't bring him any closer to why Peter Dacso had been killed, but he thought the news that the kid was clean would be enough to placate the old man for now. Ruby would have to coach Dacso along, so as not to arouse suspicion by having him drop his squalling too soon, but that could be managed.

Ruby burst out into the frigid air and began jogging in the direction of the streetcar line. As he passed the alley behind the club he heard the scrape of shoe leather on cold stone coming from the shadowed recesses. Before he could react, a gabardine octopus pinned his arms with four of its own. A fifth clamped a sweaty palm across his mouth while a sixth smashed a gun butt behind his ear. Ruby sagged and, moaning, was hauled to a waiting sedan. Shadowed figures dumped him into the trunk and banged the lid shut. Exhaust plumed in time to the roar of the engine and the car sped off.

Ice cold water hit Ruby in the face and the tiny icicles slicing into his skin brought him awake with a start. A faceless ghost was hovering over him, two eyes glaring at him. Ruby blinked and tried again and the ghostly figure became a man with two bloodshot brown eyes glaring through the eyeholes cut into the sheet over his head.

"He's coming around," the ghost announced.

"Good. I've got places to be," a bodiless voice complained.

Ruby pulled his eyes off the ghost leaning over him and cast his gaze about. A cracked ceiling overhead, another ghost leaning back precariously on a chair to the right of the bed Ruby lay on. There was a package of opened saltines and the pitcher they'd doused him with on the nightstand near the tottering ghost. Ruby became aware of a musty odor. When he tried to move its source was revealed. They'd put a canvas tent over him and tied it tight to the legs of the bed. Only his head and neck were exposed.

The ghost leaning over him slapped him hard across the face to get his attention.

"The place to your liking?" he asked. "Or should I have the bellhop collect your bags?"

Ruby just glared.

"Get on with it!" that distant voice sounded again. Ruby turned his head to the side and saw a third ghost sitting on the edge of a desk across the room near the door. Bare walls, dusty curtains... They had brought him to a closed up business so they could use the back room which served as an office/bedroom for the former owner.

The ghost over him held up a pair of leather gloves in one hand and a switchblade in the other. "Choose."

Ruby could barely contain his relief. The cold stab of fear he'd felt upon waking gradually faded with each passing second. The fact that the ghosts kept their faces covered around him and the elaborate interrogation set up meant they weren't going to kill him. Ruby needed to get this over with.

"Is that all?" Ruby growled. "I was afraid you fucking pansies were going to try and cram your pencil dicks up my arse."

The reaction was immediate. The ghost leaning over the bed stiffened while the one leaning back in the chair paused his rocking for a split second. The ghost perched on the desk brayed laughter and slapped the desk top.

The ghost who'd said 'choose' whipped his head around to look over his shoulder. "You like that? Then you take the girl and risk getting pinched as she squalls." He threw the switchblade at the other ghost's head and the man almost fell off the desk avoiding it. "Make it slow. Dice her up!" The ghost loomed over Ruby again. "Thanks for choosing, friend. Makes it more fun that way. But you didn't do that secretary of yours any favors."

The ghost near the door hopped off the desk, retrieved the switchblade and slammed the door shut so hard on the way out that the window moved. So much for screaming for help, Ruby mused. They'd picked the spot carefully.

The nearest ghost slid the leather gloves over his big, horny hands. The leather creaked as he made sure they were snug.

"I prefer it this way," the ghost said. Then he straddled Ruby and went to work.

The first few punches stung like the devil and Ruby could feel his face tighten beneath broken skin. No questions came with them and this confused the private investigator until the ghost by the window spoke. "You're lucky a dead shamus isn't on the menu just now, pal."

"Dead like that cop you killed? Dacso?" Ruby burbled between bloody lips. His vision had a black tinge at the edges and his head lolled.

"Don't know anything about any dead cop, friend." The ghost jabbed Ruby again. "We're just teaching a washed up flatfoot to keep his nose out of things that aren't his concern."

The ghost stopped the beating, climbed off the bed and pulled at the bloody gloves. Ruby's face was swollen, tight and bleeding as he held out hope that they were done with him. However the guy doing the work relished it too much and the smile stretching the cloth over his head as he peeled off the gloves meant that this was only the end of round one. Ruby took the break to thrash around in agony that was not hard to embellish. He already knew they had taken his guns by the absence of weight in the small rigs on his lower back and thigh. He slid his hand to his back pocket and found the folding hunting knife he kept there. They'd missed it. Whether out of sloppiness or a need for haste, Ruby didn't know or care. His consciousness flickering in and out, he struggled to slide the knife free without the ghosts catching the movement. The bastard they'd thrown out was after Edie!

The ghost had the gloves off now and wadded them up into a ball he tossed into the corner narrowly missing the rocking ghost. A set of brass knuckles went around the fat sausage fingers.

"Now that we've finished tenderizing," the ghost said. "Let's really go to town."

Ruby had the knife open. He went into his act. "No more, please! I beg you! I can't take no more!"

Even though Ruby couldn't see the ghost's features, he sensed the man under the sheet was disappointed. He put one knee on the bed anyway, determined to finish the job.

"Wait! Look, I know something you don't know. I – I think you busted my jaw!"

"It ain't broke," the teetering ghost said. "Yet."

"No! I'll... I'll trade!" Ruby blubbered. "I'll give you what I know and you let me go! What do you say?"

This seemed to amuse the ghost. "Sure, spill."

Ruby lowered his voice to a whisper. "Oh, it hurts! My jaw's broke sure! I can't talk. Lean down a bit. I'll be able to say it once."

The ghost leaned down six inches and Ruby could see the humor in the man's eyes. He was enjoying himself.

Ruby stabbed the knife through the tent canvas and into the man's gut.

The keen blade was angled and slid through the skin upward under the ribs. Blood exploded out of the man's mouth and the front of the sheet was instantly vivid red.

Ruby shoved the dying man aside and drove the blade into the knee of the rocking ghost who was momentarily frozen by what had transpired. The man cried out and the back of the chair smacked against the wall. One hand feverishly clutched the hilt of the knife while the other pawed futilely under the tangled folds of the sheet for a piece. Ruby seized up the empty water pitcher and smashed it down on the man's head. Jagged shards of broken glass dotted the sheet like a crown of thorns and blood started to soak into the sheet. The chair slid all the way to the floor. Ruby planted the heel of his shoe in the man's covered face. Once. Twice. The man lay still.

Ruby retrieved the knife and careened drunkenly to the door. Blackness well up around him and he pitched headlong, scraping his battered flesh along the wooden floor. Groggy, desperate, he rose up and leaned against the wall next to the door. He fumbled with the handle, got it open and stumbled down a short hallway to a street exit. On the way, he realized he'd forgotten to look for his guns or take the one the rocking ghost had made a play for. He could barely keep his eyes focused after the beating he'd endured and oblivion hovered like a hornet looking for a soft spot to strike. Ruby dared not risk going back.

He broke the window of their car with a garbage can, yanked the door open and fell across the seat. He hotwired it and the engine thrummed. Stomping on the pedals, he threw the car into gear and barrelled out of the alley.

"I'm coming, Edie!" he roared and slurred. "I'm coming!"

Edie Adams lived on the fringe between good and bad neighborhoods. Ruby blacked out on the way and ploughed the grill of the Hudson into a newsstand. Cursing the heavens and the earth, he threw the thing into reverse and got out of the tangle of broken wood and scattered magazines. He stamped down on the clutch, worked the gears and resumed shoving his way through traffic until he reached her building where he skidded to a stop and fell out onto the snowy roadway. He wore no jacket and icy slush soaked him to the skin. The cold snow soothed his throbbing face but did not dampen the fire in his heart.

Slipping and sliding, he was up again and skating towards the entrance.

"Blood exploded out of the man's mouth..."

He had a key to the place and used it. She lived on the second floor. Ruby had to lean against the banister while his eyes adjusted to the bright lights of the foyer. He shook his head and that black tide rose up again. He had to catfoot it up there or Edie was done for. Leaning heavily on the banister, he placed his feet carefully on the carpeted stairwell and started to climb.

He did not remember the climb but suddenly found himself on the second floor landing. Edie's flop was down three doors on the left. Ruby lost count on the way but recognized the large, heavy crucifix Edie hung there to ward off evil. Only it hadn't worked this time, Angel, had it?

The lock had been forced. Ruby eased inside and almost knocked over an umbrella stand.

They were in the bedroom. The night table light was on and there was the ghost leaning over Edie tied to the bed with stockings. Ruby sidled up to the half-open door. If the ghost tipped to his presence there was no telling what the son of a bitch would do.

Ruby flattened up against the wall and turned to peer around the jamb. The bastard had cut away Edie's nightgown. A plum-colored mouse had swelled up under one of her eyes, her lip was split. That did it for Ruby.

Bellowing, he charged into the room, the iron crucifix from the front door raised in his fist. He brought it down on the side of the ghost's head as the man turned and there was a wet thump. Ruby felt the impact vibrate up his arm. The ghost dropped like a stone across Edie's nude form.

"I got you, Angel!" Ruby swayed as he slashed at her bonds with the knife. "I'm here, baby." The crucifix clunked to the floor. Then Ruby pitched senseless across the end of the bed.

He was awake instantly. Or so he thought. He sprawled in the arm chair near the bed and Adams was in the bath robe he had bought her for her birthday. She was mopping his puffy face with warm water, her touch as gentle as a pleasant thought.

"Angel!" Ruby snapped. "You okay?"

Adams nodded. "This isn't the first time I've been knocked around, although it's been awhile. I'll live."

Ruby motioned with his chin at the ghost laying face down on the bed.

"He's breathing, barely," Adams said. "You walloped him pretty hard."

"He had it coming." Ruby gently pushed the warm, red rag in Adams's hand aside and squirmed out of the chair.

"You've got to take it easy," she cautioned. "Your face looks like an old catcher's mitt."

"No time. You've got a safe place you can go?"

Adams said she did as she came up off one knee.

"Okay. Help me tie this skunk up, then get over there. Don't tell anyone where you're going. Not even me." Ruby headed unsteadily for the door. "I'm going to see about the old man, then bring Mac in all the way. We're finished with this one."

When the ghost was gagged and tightly bound, Ruby turned to leave but stopped at the door and came back. He gently cupped the girl's face in one rough palm and his eyes moved over her injuries. "You don't belong in this world, Angel."

Adams smiled through swollen lips but there was pain in her eyes. "It's the only game in town."

The Dacsos lived on the second floor of a three-storey walk up next to the Rumrunner bar on 43rd. Ruby slid the vehicle in at the corner and tumbled out to walk back to the old man's place. The lock on the street door was broken and Ruby feared the worst until he shifted so that the dim light over the door could fall on the lock and saw that the damage was old and hadn't been repaired. He pushed through. Dacso had gotten under his skin somehow and Ruby would never forgive himself if anything happened to the old codger.

He pounded up the narrow flight of steps. Dacso's door was right at the turn to the hallway leading to the next flight. He tried the door handle and it revolved only halfway. The lock was tight. Ruby pounded on the door and to hell with the neighbors.

He saw a light go on under the door.

"Come on, Dacso, it's me!" he shouted. "We've got things to do."

The lock clacked like a pistol shot and Dacso opened the door. He was in shorts and an undershirt. An open robe hung loosely on his spare frame.

"Get dressed. I've got a car downstairs."

"Good Lord!" Dacso gasped at the state of Ruby's features. "What happened to you?"

"No time! Move!"

Ruby ignored Dacso's questions until they were in the car and back on the road.

"Tell me!" Dacso demanded for the thousandth time. "What has happened? Have you learned something about my boy?"

"I've learned plenty, but you've got to do something for me first."

"What? Anything!"

"I want you to look at some faces first. Then we'll talk."

Minutes later Ruby turned into the alley and jerked the car to a halt at the door through which he'd escaped the sadistic ghosts. He led Dacso inside after looking through the window to see that both ghosts were still there and to make sure no one was keeping them company. The place was quiet. On the way in, Ruby found his coat draped over the back of a chair. There was no sign of his guns.

Dacso hesitated at the threshold of the office/bedroom. Ruby checked the guy laying in a heap at the window. He was still snoring through a mashed nose. There was no reason to check the guy with the fists. He yanked the sheet off the living ghost and the man's head was sheathed in darkness.

"You know this clown?" Ruby barked at Dacso.

Dacso jumped and Ruby could see the man force his gaze to look at the bloody head. From where he stood, Dacso could not see the man's features as his head lolled in a shadowed corner beneath the window sill.

Ruby could either drag Dacso into the room or haul the body out of the corner to the end of the bed where the streetlight shone through the window. Actually there was a third alternative.

He dropped the sheet over the bleeding form and reached the dead ghost in two strides. He yanked off the sheet covering the corpse and bright light shone on the man's death rictus of a face. "How about this one?"

Dacso was even more appalled but he ratcheted his head around to stare down at the form lying in a heap at the foot of the bed.

"I've never see him before," he said.

"You're sure? Maybe your son knew him?" Ruby persisted. "Ever bring him around the house?"

Mention of his son galvanized Dacso and he stepped quickly into the room to scrutinize the face of the corpse more closely. "The face is unfamiliar. I've never seen this man before."

"Shit!" Ruby said. He looked out the window then at Dacso. "I threw your son at them when they were giving me the business and they denied knowing him. They were smooth about it. I was hoping they were lying." He came over and stood facing Dacso. "Here's the straight dope. Your son was working undercover, trying to expose cops on the take. This is how it works: rackets buy cops in their territories and get a free pass for their money. A snake named Leo Shairp runs your son's beat. Only he's got competition from the Sanfori syndicate trying to muscle in and whoever bids the highest gets the pass. The straight cops were hoping the bidding war would pull the dirty cops out of the woodwork to make a grab and your son would be there to finger them when they showed. But it all went to hell. What I can't figure out is how."

Dacso sagged and Ruby had to grab him to keep him from hitting the floor. He guided the old man to the foot of the bed.

"My boy," Dacso whispered. "My good boy. I knew. I knew it all along."

Ruby let the poor guy babble as he went down on one knee to paw at the dead man's clothes in search of a wallet. He went over the beating in his mind. The ghosts had merely been trying to scare him off their action. That made sense as far as it went. But it didn't bring him any closer to discovering who had killed Peter Dacso. If these ghosts were Sanfori's boys, killing a cop would hardly earn them any favors with their new guardians. Something was missing.

Then he found it.

Ruby fished into the jacket pocket of the dead man and felt a familiar heaviness. His blood froze in his veins and an icicle of dread sliced along his spine. He pulled out the creased leather folder, opened it and stared down at the gold, NYPD detective's badge inside.

The dead ghost was a cop. Ruby had killed a cop in his mad flight.

The breath hissed out from between his clamped lips and he rubbed the back of his neck as he tried to sort the thing out. There was going to be hell to pay.

Meanwhile Dacso had become hypnotized by the sight of the dead body at his feet. His eyes widened and his lips trembled. All the color drained out of his face and he began to slide off the bed. Ruby, lost in thought, heard the rustling sound and caught Dacso on the way down. The man was a bag of sticks and Ruby placed him back on the bed.

"I had hoped to never see such things again!" Dacso said, his gaze once more riveted on the corpse. "But it never goes away. Rivers of blood spilling out all over. War with Germany will turn rivers into oceans. Please, Lord, not again."

Ruby knew what the old man was saying. It got to you sometimes. "Easy, Pops."

Dacso's hands fluttered on his thighs and his eyes blinked as if he had awakened from a trance.

"Forgive a foolish old man," he said with a weak attempt at a smile. "This terrible sight has re-opened old wounds."

"Take a minute to catch your breath."

"It will take until Judgment Day for me to catch my breath." He stared down at the sprawled ghost, the clawed fingers clutching at the red-stained sheet. "In the war I killed men in this way. They haunt me from time to time."

"Put it out of your mind. Your son is in the clear. Focus on that."

But Dacso did not hear Ruby's advice. "One dead man is my constant torment. We had done our duty in battle, then we lay down our weapons. It was Christmas-time, enemies became friends, and I sat with a man I had so gravely wounded. I told him I was sorry for what I'd done. I would have lain down my life if I could take back the pain I had inflicted, but it was too late. It is always too late. I gave him my bayonet, the one I had plunged into him only a few hours before. I begged him to use it on me. He refused."

Ruby stood staring down at Dacso. His mind whirled, pin-balling between acceptance and denial of what he had just heard. He was numb, he could not move, couldn't think. It was impossible. It couldn't be true.

Ruby's voice was a weak croak. "W-where was this?"

"France," Dacso whispered. He could not pull his gaze off the dead man. "Soissons."

The world tilted like the deck of a ship in a gale. Ruby stumbled to his feet, away from the bed and the old man. His back slammed into the door jamb. A look of horror twisted his hard, battered features, his eyes saucer-wide, staring at something too deep to fathom. He bolted.

It can't be true! Ruby screamed in his thoughts. *It wasn't true!* Dacso could not be the man he'd loathed all of his adult life. The old man could not be the one he'd imagined killing in a thousand hideous ways for tearing his father from him. He couldn't be!

But what were the odds! The same battlefield at Christmas! The lingering stab wound! Damned Hungary had fought on the German side!

Ruby couldn't think. He moved to throw the car into gear and realized he still clutched the dead ghost's bloody sheet in his hand. He tossed it onto the passenger seat and got the machine moving. The car roared up the avenues blindly under his guidance. He didn't know what to do! What to feel! Salty tears burned down into the cuts on his face and he pawed the moisture away. This started the wounds bleeding again and blood mixed with the tears. He could feel his sanity teetering on the brink. Things were starting to whirl, and if he didn't find something to grab onto in the mael-strom he was through. He'd killed a dirty cop because of Dacso and now his ass was in a wringer. The boys in blue didn't take kindly to cop kill-ers and unless he could find undeniable proof the killing was justified, he was as good as dead. He pounded the steering wheel in frustration as he hunted for an angle.

Shairp!

There was the key to the whole rotten mess! Dacso Jr. had been killed in the building Leo Shairp let his no-account brother run and the Shairp syndicate was desperate to hold their territory. It was the only place Ruby could think of to start looking and, more importantly, get his mind off the old man.

He left the car near Washington Square Park and hotfooted along the icy sidewalk to Shairp's building and around back. Ruby did not know what room Leo Shairp had stuck his brother in, but the fire escape would get him inside the building without the goons at the front tipping to his presence.

There was muscle in the alley. Ruby had driven past the place and had had a glance on the way by. The night was bitterly cold and a light snowfall floated gently down. Through the gauze of snow and the fogged passenger window, he'd seen two goons at the far end of the alley huddled over a burning trash barrel, winking at the blaze while extending numb fingers towards the flames. The fire escape was at the opposite end of the alley, close to the street Ruby used for his approach. If he could get up onto the metal gangway with a modicum of quiet, they'd be too far away to hear or see anything. That was his hope anyway.

He crept around the corner of the building, the accumulated snow muf-fled his hard heels. With a spring, he was up and curled his fingers around the ladder. The snow cushioned the sound of the ladder coming down with a barely audible screech. Ruby was up the stairs in a heartbeat.

A window was open a crack on the second floor. Ruby couldn't believe his luck but went with it. The reason behind the open window became ap-parent after he had eased it up and climbed through. It was stiflingly hot in the building, the metal radiators steamed like molten steel and the window had been left open for a cross draft. Ruby gently closed the window behind him. He paused and slipped on the ghost sheet from the car. The last thing he needed was for Shairp or his boys to be able to ID him. He smoothed the sheet with its large irregular blood stain across the stomach and crept up the carpeted hallway.

The first door he came to had a lot of male voices behind it talking loud-ly—probably an all-night poker game involving Shairp's servants. Ruby continued on.

There was a toilet in the middle of the hall, a narrow room judging by the width of the door. That door was open and light spilled out into the cor-ridor. Whoever was on the crapper had left the door ajar to catch the wisp of cross breeze. Without it the bathroom would have been a steam bath. Ruby unfolded his hunting knife and crouched to spring. If the clown on the pot managed to shout out, Ruby was sunk. He waited until he heard the guy moving around. The smell drifting out into the corridor told him the man had finished and the roll of the spool was Ruby's signal.

He lunged through the door and caught the guy reaching across his body for the paper while his other clutched his open trousers. Ruby jabbed the knife at the guy's throat while clamping a hand over the startled 'O' of the goon's mouth at the sight of a lunatic ghost in front of him. The guy got the message and did not struggle.

Ruby removed the free hand but pressed the blade a little deeper into the man's unshaven throat. Reaching behind, Ruby found the shoulder rig the guy had hung on the back of the door and yanked the revolver free. He exchanged the knife for the gun as a means to keep the guy quiet and had one question.

"Shairp's little brother. Where?"

The man's eyes swung up once and to the right and back two times in rapid succession. Next floor. Second door down. Ruby got the message but needed to be sure. He shook his head and placed the maw of the revolver between the man's eyes. A fresh jet of urine splashed in the bowl and the man's breathing became labored and frantic under Ruby's hand. The guy repeated the eye movements and ended this time with an emphatic nod. Ruby removed the barrel.

The guy then pleaded with those same eyes, indicating he'd like to get dressed before whatever happened next. A corner of Ruby's mouth curled up under the sheet and he nodded once quickly, stepping back half a pace. The guy's shoulders slumped in relief and he bent over slightly to retrieve his pants. Ruby laid the butt of the revolver behind the man's ear and caught him as he dropped off the toilet. Ruby eased him down to the cold tile. He left the light on and closed the door. It was his hope that he'd be long gone before the guy regained consciousness.

Ruby followed the direction and tried the door to Shairp's room. It was unlocked. Looks like the Shairps had a lot of faith in their goons, he mused.

He stepped gingerly inside.

The bedroom was off a large sitting room and Ruby could see Shairp's wasted form barely making a tent of the blankets. His lusty snores covered Ruby's approach. Standing over the sleeping form, he put the gun in Shairp's face and clapped a hand around the scrawny throat.

Shairp's eyes flew open and he thrashed at the sight of the gun in the fist of a blood-stained figure towering over him. Ruby shook his head slowly and Shairp quieted down. Keeping the gun on the prone form, Ruby dropped into the arm chair near the bed. He showed Shairp the gun and the big Adam's apple in the shrivelled chicken neck went up and down. Ruby next showed him the hunting knife and stuck it point first into the nightstand within easy reach.

Ruby unloaded the gun, the six cartridges clacked together in his lap.

"Every lie, I load one cartridge," he whispered to Shairp. "And we play Russian roulette."

Shairp stared in mute horror.

"Who set Peter Dacso up?" Ruby hissed.

Shairp shook his head and whispered dryly. "I don't know no Dacso."

Ruby palmed one of the bullets and made a show of loading it into an empty chamber. It snapped home on the piece and Ruby gave it a spin. He lunged forward, clamped a hand over Shairp's mouth put the gun to the man's forehead and pulled the trigger.

Click.

Shairp's bodied arched, then collapsed. Ruby sat back down again and watched Shairp struggle to get his lungs working again.

"Who set Dacso up?"

"I don't know any names," Shairp rasped.

Play time was over. Ruby loaded a cartridge. Shairp thought it was the second to go in and flailed when Ruby repeated the spin of the cylinder and choked off the man's air.

Click.

"I tell ya I don't know!" Shairp croaked.

"Why was he bumped off?" Ruby asked from the chair.

"Payoff," Shairp wheezed.

"It had something to do with the payoff to dirty cops?"

Shairp hesitated, reluctant to rat out his brother.

Ruby loaded another cartridge. Spun. Aimed.

Shairp's arm thrust out imploringly. "Wait! Wait!" he croaked. "Leo sent the payment over with the kid. A hundred gees! Only he vanished and so did the money."

Ruby reloaded the remaining cartridges. "And?"

"I swear I don't know. I only got the dope afterwards. The three cops who were supposed to pick up the payoff banged on my door and told me to torch the building. That was all they said. Torch the place!"

"You knew Dacso was on the third floor!"

"No! I didn't know what the hell was going on. Neither did Lou. The money was gone and Lou wanted the kid's balls to hang on his tree."

Ruby had overstayed his welcome. He smashed the gun barrel across Shairp's pale temple and got the hell out of the building. He tossed the sheet into the gutter outside and sprinted for the car.

Back on the road, Ruby tried to piece together what had happened after the kid had left with the money for the meet. Ruby had not seen a suitcase with the kid when he'd been yanked off the fire escape. And who had done the yanking? The Shairp crowd were out. That left the cops.

Which meant –

Ruby floored the accelerator.

The car sluiced in the snow and slush, bumping the curb outside the old man's house. The light was out in the second floor window, which suited Ruby. He didn't want to deal with the old man just then. He kicked in Dacso's door and moved about in the dark rooms. The kid's bedroom was at the end of a short hallway. Ruby burst into it taking in the unmade bed and dirty laundry strewn about. He started tearing the place apart dumping drawers, ransacking the closet, flipping the soiled mattress. Ruby had about given up, half convinced he'd missed something along the way. Then he saw that a join between two floorboards wasn't quite flush. He dove over the skewed mattress and pried at the gap with the tip of the knife. It popped up and there was the case.

Ruby pulled it loose and put it on the dresser. He broke the lock and there were the stacks of used bills in all denominations. A manila envelope sat atop the heap. Inside was a passport with a phony name to go with Peter Dacso's mug. A train ticket to Montreal made out in that phony name completed the picture.

"I'll be goddamned!" Ruby said to the empty room. "The kid was pulling a double-cross."

It all made sense to him now. The kid had gotten the trust of the Shairp crowd, took the payoff but had to hoodwink the cops waiting for it long enough to buy time to scram across the border before they got wise and used their authority to render escape impossible. Only they caught up with him on that deserted street. Maybe they were shadowing him, maybe they'd been tipped. There was no way the kid could have known. He climbed up that fire escape with his fellow officers without a care in the world. Until they got to the third-story window. Then he'd gotten nervous. By then it was too late. They hacked him up so he'd give them the location of the stolen money and burned the building down around him.

But why hadn't they taken the money?

Because they knew Lou Shairp was on the hunt for it.

So they bided their time. They had the location, the kid was out of the picture, all they had to do was wait for things to quiet down between Shairp and the ghosts, maybe taking a pay off from the sheet camp if they could pay the most, and the hundred gees would be gravy. The crooked cops knew they could always pin the kid's murder on the ghosts and look like angels with Shairp's bunch in the process.

It was a sweet deal.

But why hadn't it worked?

The old man. He kept shooting his mouth off, stirring up the dust as fast as it could settle. So they'd dressed up like ghosts to discourage Ruby from making matters worse. The funny thing here, Ruby mused, was that they didn't know an invisible dragnet was closing in on them the whole time.

What about the old man anyway? He hadn't forgotten who Alexei Dacso was. And here was a way to get him back for his past crimes, for all the unshakable misery he'd inflicted on Ruby these last twenty years. It would kill Dacso to learn that his son, his good boy, was nothing but a rotten crook trying to make off with a big score while leaving others to die for it. Peter Dacso wasn't worth spit. Here was Ruby's revenge and it was a fitting one. Dacso had it coming.

Ruby picked up the phone and dialed the number for the station.

McGinnis led Ruby and Adams out of his office. "Thanks both of you for stopping by to make statements. The D.A's gonna be handing down a passle of indictments. The Shairp syndicate is going the way of the dodo."

They moved up the center aisle between the rows of desks and Ruby caught the odd dirty look from some of the detectives. So did McGinnis.

"Don't sweat it, Rick," he said. "Those two dirty cops masquerading as ghosts have both cut deals, blaming the dead one, Petrie, for the murders

of the three real ghosts out on Lafayette. They did us a favor in that regard as it sent Sanfori packing. He's convinced Shairp ordered the hit. The
ghosts have also both sworn out statements that you acted in self defense
killing Petrie. They would have sworn statements to just about anything to
save their rotten necks but we held them to the truth."

"Yeah, I heard as much from the shyster representing me," Ruby admit-
ted. "But law and justice are two different things, and I don't know if any
of these yahoos are contemplating taking matters into their own hands."

"Everyone here knows the score," McGinnis said. "The Captain made
sure of that. You haven't made any friends, but you'll skate, trust me."

"I'll believe it when I see it. What about the kid?"

"They're telling tales about that. They say it was Petrie did the slice job
while they set up the burn."

"They say why they did the kid?" Ruby asked.

"Yeah, but it's a crock," McGinnis replied. "According to them, the kid
stole the payoff money and they took him up to that room to get where
he'd hidden it out of him. They say Petrie got the location while they were
out of earshot and that he held it over them to keep them from getting
funny ideas. We don't believe a word of it. My guess is they learned the
kid was working for us and wanted to send a message. Also, torching one
of Shairp's places was to let Lou Shairp see what could happen if he didn't
come across with more of the long green in light of Sanfori's interest in the
territory. Another message. Pure and simple. Well, they'll do twenty in the
big house, rather than get the chair, for killing the kid. That's our reply to
their message."

They were at the top of the stairs. "Be seeing ya, Mac." Ruby said.

Downstairs Ruby insisted Adams do the driving as he'd had enough of
what passed for motoring in the city. They piled in and Adams got the car
moving.

"Did you stash the money like I told you?" Ruby asked.

"Safe as houses."

"Okay. Remember now, not too much to each mission at any one time.
We've got to dole it out careful or it'll raise eyebrows."

"I know, boss. We went over it."

Ruby leaned back and gazed out the window.

"You did the right thing with Mr. Dacso," Adams said at last. "Keeping
quiet about the boy."

Ruby waved that away. "If the money turned up, what's left of Shairp's
bunch would come for the old man and the stooge who helped him. Name-

ly, me. I didn't do it for old man Dacso."

"Like hell you didn't," she insisted. "Besides, never mind the money. You left him his son's untarnished memory when you didn't come forward. And he's so happy to have the thing settled, you'll be getting free meat deliveries from now until Judgment Day."

They stopped at a light. The sky was a vast expanse of cotton wool that promised more snow before evening. A newsie brayed out the headlines. The war in Europe was not going well. The Japs had their sabres out and if you listened close you could hear them rattling. Ruby guessed it wouldn't be long now.

Adams seemed to read his thoughts. "We've got to enjoy the peace while it lasts," she said. "You should be proud you brought some to that nice old man. He's suffered enough."

"He's not alone."

"Don't be like that, Rick," she scolded. "We've all got our crosses to bear, and none is any heavier or lighter than the next guy's. We're all equal under heaven."

"This ain't heaven, Angel," Ruby observed, the newsie's barked warning trailing them as they accelerated through the intersection. "This ain't heaven."

The End

MINING A RUBY

I love hardboiled fiction.

From Cornell Woolrich, Mickey Spillane, Dashiell Hammett, Raymond Chandler, Brett Halliday and John D. MacDonald to Dan J. Marlowe, Donald Hamilton and Edward S. Aarons and so many more, I gorged on hardboiled mysteries long before I stumbled upon Doc Savage, who led me to the hero pulps.

So when I first heard about hardboiled private eye Rick Ruby being conjured into existence by Bobby Nash and Sean Taylor, my mouth began to water. It sounded like a great project and a lot of fun. However, at the time Rick Ruby was taking shape and a character bible was being hammered out, I was deep into researching a pulp novel featuring German heroes while at the same time lending Mark Halegua a helping hand in putting the finishing touches on the first story featuring his own creation, the Red Badge. As much as I wanted to be a part of the first Ruby anthology, I felt there was no way I could switch gears and do a tale.

Then Airship 27 made me an offer I couldn't refuse. While I plodded along with those other projects, our intrepid Air Chief, Ron Fortier, went out and recruited Mark Wheatley to do the fantastic cover which graces the book and Rob Moran to do the wonderful interior illustrations you've been enjoying as you made it this far into the book. Well, when I heard this news, what had already been a dream project suddenly became too good to be true with the additions of two mega-talented artists! As two story spots in the book had not yet been finalized, I realized I had a chance to be part of something really special.

But, like any good pulp story, there was a race against time.

You see, three writers (myself included) were competing for the last TWO spots behind Bobby's and Sean's efforts. Ron, God love 'im, had long ago instituted a 'first come, first served' policy when it comes to story submissions for Airship 27's pulp anthologies. This was done to be fair to everyone involved and to keep books from languishing if one story was late for whatever reason. Therefore, if I could write my story and get it in ahead of my distinguished competition, I had a shot at making the final cut. Well, any pulp writer worth his or her salt has to be able to churn out purple prose, win that race against the clock. All I had to do was get cracking.

Shouldn't be a problem for an old word-slinger like me, right?

The problem was that I was coming to the project months behind others who'd expressed interest in contributing. As far as I knew, these fine folks were putting the finishing touches on their tales while I wrestled with the Muse for an idea so I could begin!

It was time to write and write fast!

What followed were seven intensely creative days. I ate, drank and slept Rick Ruby over that period, scribbling the whole time at a feverish pace. Every morning I'd check my email dreading word that the other would-be contributors had submitted their tales before I could finish, and my effort would be put aside for future volumes in the series. This would not have been the end of the world of course, but I felt so much like a pulp writer of old, and was having so much fun banging out pages, that I hoped I could see the project through and reach the finish line in time. Fortunately, I had not used my hardboiled voice since writing my Pulp Ark Award-nominated tale, 'Run,' and the words poured out tough as nails as I tore along and the pages piled up.

In the end, luck was on my side. I finished the tale and sent it off with fingers crossed. Somehow I managed to get away with not breathing for an hour or two as I awaited word on my tale's fate. Did it get in on time? Did the Air Chief like it?

I received a resounding 'yes' to both these questions and I could breathe again.

And now here is the tale for you, dear reader, to peruse. I aimed for a heaping dose of Spillane, seasoned with a touch of James Ellroy and spiced with just a dash of Wold-Newton. Those are the elements that went into my meat grinder of a brain anyway. What you just read is what came out. I hope you found it to your liking.

I want to thank Ron for the opportunity to participate in the book. It was a lot of fun and an honor to share pages with such great talent. And yet we've barely scratched the surface of the great characters Bobby and Sean gave us. If you enjoyed the book, please drop Ron a line to tell him so. Or, better yet, post a review on Amazon.com or your personal blog. Airship 27 aims to please, and if fans want more Rubys, we word-miners will head back down into the stygian depths and see what jewels we can pry out of the cold earth. It'll be a pleasure.

ANDREW SALMON - is the winner of a Pulp Factory Award for his first Sherlock Holmes story, "The Adventure of the Locked Room" (*Sherlock Holmes Consulting Detective: Volume One*), and has received nominations for the Arthur Ellis Award (the equivalent of the Edgar in his native Canada) as well as Pulp Ark Award and Pulp Factory Award consideration for various tales. His work has appeared in numerous magazines, including *Masked Gun Mystery, Planetary Stories, Parsec, Storyteller, TBT* and *Thirteen Stories.*

He is creating a Brand/X superhero serial novel currently running in *A Thousand Faces Magazine* (to read the saga to date, see issues #0, 2, 3, 5, 7, and 12 which are all still available).

He has published or appeared in fourteen books: *The Forty Club* (which Midwest Book Reviews calls "a good solid little tale you will definitely carry with you for the rest of your life"), *The Light Of Men,* which has been called "a book of such immense significance that it is not only meant to be read, but also to be experienced... a work of grim power" – C. Saunders. *Secret Agent X: Volume One* and *Three, Ghost Squad: Rise of the Black Legion* (with Ron Fortier), *Jim Anthony Super Detective: Volume One, Sherlock Holmes Consulting Detective: Volumes One, Two* and *Three, Dan Fowler G-Man: Volume One, Black Bat Mystery: Volume One, Mars McCoy Space Ranger: Volume. One,* a completely revised edition of *The Dark Land* ("a straight out science-fiction thriller that fires on all cylinders" – Pulp Fiction Reviews) and *The Ruby Files: Volume One* constitute his work for Airship 27 to date.

Andrew's work will also appear in the upcoming *Mystery Men and Women: Volume Two* (with Mark Halegua) – from Airship 27.

To learn more about his work check out the following links:

http://www.amazon.com/Andrew-Salmon/e/B002NS5KR0/ref=ntt_athr_dp_pel_pop_2.

http://stores.lulu.com/airship27
http://airship27hangar.com
www.lulu.com/AndrewSalmon
www.lulu.com/thousand-faces

THE CASE OF THE WAYWARD BROTHER

By Bobby Nash

Richard Ruby was having one of those days.

After the hassles he'd already faced that afternoon, and they had been numerous, the only thing he had wanted from his evening was to be left alone to drink until he couldn't see straight. And he really wanted to do so in peace. He was in no mood to be sociable, not even to the regulars whom he saw nightly. He had decided to start slow and was on his third beer since he had bellied up to his usual spot at the bar. The brew was cold and stung the fresh split in his lip, and he winced every time the bottle touched it. One more and he would switch to the hard stuff.

After a few quick *"Hey! How are yous?"* and hurried excuses about being late and in a hurry, he made a beeline for his usual spot at the bar where he had shared a few words with the bartender, his friend, Bruce Strickland, a rail thin man that everyone called Broom Stick. Before Rick, the abbreviated name by which his friends called him, had even taken his seat, Broom Stick dropped the first bottle of beer on the polished oak at the far end of the bar where he always perched. A student of human nature, he noted Rick's mood right off and went ahead and dropped a second open bottle in front of him before he asked for it. Rick assumed his friend could easily read his mood and reacted accordingly. Broom Stick was the manager, bartender, stock boy, handyman, and all-around jack-of-all-trades at Belle's, which would have been Rick's regular haunt even if he weren't on the payroll. Although Belle's was a jazz club, calling it just a jazz club seemed a disservice not only to the grand old building that the place called its home, but also to the club's owner, May Belle Williams, another friend of his.

The office that housed his private investigation business was just upstairs,

46

but it wasn't all that unusual for Rick to conduct business while sidled up to the bar as the sweet jazz music serenaded him. The laid back atmosphere of the club had also eased a client through bad news on more than one occasion. After downing his first two beers quickly, the P. I. nursed his third while Evelyn Johnson belted out a throaty jazz standard on the stage. As usual, when Evelyn sang, he got lost in the sound of her angelic voice and the world around him vanished in a smoky haze. However, it was when she was offstage that he got lost in the rest of her. Rick could easily drown in Evelyn's deep brown eyes as he caressed her long, slender legs that felt like satin to the touch. Rick would buy her a drink once her set was finished, if he was still sober enough.

Rick liked to sit at the far end of the bar. He told everyone it was his favorite seat, but the truth of the matter was that it was the best seat in the house because from that perch he could easily see the entirety of Belle's main room. In his line of work you weren't considered successful unless you made yourself an enemy or twelve.

And Rick was quite successful.

Except for those odd occasions when he shared a private booth with one of the ladies or a client, Rick Ruby took up his normal perch at the end of the bar. There were far more comfortable places to sit, but he believed it would look pretty bad on his resume if he got caught off guard while crying over a beer. Such a thing would be bad for business so he never sat with his back to the room. Any room. Even the desk in his office was situated so he had a clear view of the outer office door. He was a cautious sort.

Rick pulled a hard drag off of a filtered cigarette while nursing his third beer of the evening. He had a headache that threatened to make his eyeballs explode. He was pretty sure that his sore eye would be a slightly darker shade in the morning and his lip would probably double in size, but at least he had gotten some satisfaction. His last client had stiffed him when it came time to settle his bill, so Rick decided to go over and see the man and offer him payment options and discuss the penalty for non-payment.

Despite a lengthy discussion that left Rick with scraped knuckles, a possible black eye, and a split lip, he still hadn't retrieved the money he was owed. Rick very much doubted that payment for services rendered would be forthcoming without a followup reminder to his client about honoring one's commitments. Even though his former client hadn't faired much better in their discussion, Rick decided that their next conversation would include a third party, a Louisville Slugger that Rick kept in the corner of his office for just such an occasion, just within arms reach of his desk. The rent was due and he needed a paying case soon or else his landlord was liable to have him kneecapped.

Or worse.

Rick swore, as he often did when he was broke, which turned out to be more often than he liked, that he should simply move into his office and be done with it. He spent more time there anyway.

"You've got a visitor, Rick," the bartender told him as he pointed toward the entrance where a woman stood, looking around the room. She was a vision in white, decked out in a floor-length black dress with a slit up one side that revealed shapely legs barely concealed beneath dark stockings. A white fur coat hung off of her shoulders like a cloak. Her demeanor spoke of money and status. While it was not unusual to see people of influence inside Belle's, they were usually a bit more discreet when they entered. That meant she wasn't here for pleasure, seeing how the other side lived, but on business as Broom Stick predicted. When her eyes fell on Rick she made a beeline for his end of the bar, which only cemented his read on her. Broom Stick was good at reading people, which was probably why he and Rick got along so well. He could see through Rick's B.S. with ease.

"Thanks, Broom Stick," Rick muttered to the bartender around the butt of the cigarette clenched between his lips. The last thing Rick was in the mood for was dealing with a client, but it had been awhile since he had any actual coin in his pocket that he could ill afford to turn away potential paying clients. Not for the first time, Rick was glad he got to drink for free at Belle's, one of the perks of his arrangement with May Belle. Rick wasn't just Belle's favorite customer, but he was also the house dick, the detective on call anytime trouble brewed or whenever May Belle Williams had need of his unique services. That meant he drank for free, which even he had to admit was a better deal for him than for the house. She was also his landlord and rented him an office and apartment dirt cheap.

Rick's potential client was stunning; not just her movie star good looks or her tight sculpted frame, but even her clothes hung on her every curve as if it had been sculpted to fit her and only her. This lady was dressed to kill. Even though she was trying hard to blend in, everything about her announced just how out of place she was in a dive like Belle's. If there was one time when attractive people tried to hide their beauty, it was when they were hiring someone like Rick Ruby. Unfortunately for her, there was no way she was not being noticed in that dress. She wore a sweet, floral fragrance that arrived ahead of her. Rick didn't normally like such a strong perfume on a woman, but she made it work.

Like every other man in the bar, Rick watched her glide across the floor in her shiny, unscathed high heels, her tight blonde curls bouncing with each elegant step. She had the walk down pat, allowing just enough wiggle to arouse without taking away from her high-class image. Rick had to guess that this was a woman more accustomed to gala premieres and social events than hanging out in a place like Belle's. With her looks and grace she had power over the male of the species, no doubt.

And she knew exactly how to use it.

"I'm Marilyn Carlyle," she said with a demure demeanor.

"Hi," Rick said, offering his best professional smile.

"You're Mr. Ruby?" she asked, which he found amusing. She had obviously done her homework since she had zeroed in on him as soon as she stepped through the door.

"Yes," he said, keeping it simple. "What can I do for you?"

"Mr. Ruby, I need your help."

The first words out of her mouth were a lie.

At least Rick was pretty sure that was the case. Broom Stick wasn't the only one who knew how to read people. Like most New Yorkers, Rick had a built-in B.S. detector that whispered in his ear when it smelled something stinky. It was screaming like a four alarmer as he listened to the lady's story.

Right off the bat, he suspected that her name was not Marilyn Carlyle. He had nothing to base that on except experience, but he trusted his instincts. They had served him well when he had been walking a beat and even more so when he made detective. When he made the move from civil servant to self-employed private investigator he found those instincts, finely honed over time, to be even more valuable. Plus, he had chosen a line of work where people lied to him on a regular basis, so he was used to being told what people thought he wanted to hear instead of the truth, especially the sort of dames that hired him. He'd only met a handful that weren't working some kind of angle. He would love it if more of his clients were nice, honest, respectable members of society, but those types of people rarely needed his type of service, so he couldn't be choosy when it came to who knocked on his door or sat beside him at the bar.

On the upside, being surrounded by so many inaccuracies and half-truths on a daily basis was enough to make any man adept at sorting truth from fiction. And Rick Ruby, private eye, was damn good at his job.

"I am very much in need of your services, Mr. Ruby," the woman who introduced herself as Marilyn Carlyle said.

Rick slid off the barstool with practiced ease and accepted the woman's outstretched hand. Her skin was silky smooth, almost like porcelain. She was a tall drink of water, almost equaling him in stature. Rick liked tall dames. There was something about a pair of long, shapely legs that made him go weak in the knees. And this woman had legs that seemed to climb forever.

"Why don't you step into my office and tell me what's bothering you, Miss Carlyle," Rick said as he ushered her toward the barstool next to his. "Can I get you a drink?"

"No. No thank you." She said it quickly.

A little too quickly, Rick thought. "So what can I do for you?" he said instead.

She hesitated a moment as if she were unsure of what to do next. "Your office is in a bar?" she asked, as so many of the clients he met inside Belle's instead of in his office upstairs did. If nothing else, meeting at the bar served as a nice icebreaker before getting down to business.

"Where better?" he answered with a boyish grin, as if that was all the explanation needed. Most people never pushed beyond that answer, which suited the P. I. just fine. The last thing Rick wanted to do was discuss his private life, such as it was, with total strangers. He still found it hard to believe that people actually came to him with their problems in the first place, but a job was a job and sometimes paid the bills, so who was he to complain?

"I..." she stammered before telling her second lie of the evening. "I see your point."

"So..." he prodded.

"I... my brother is... missing. I want you to find him for me."

Rick jotted down the word *"brother?"* with a question mark on the flip pad he kept in his shirt pocket. Early in his career in the private sector he discovered that many clients lost confidence in a P. I. that wrote his notes on a cocktail napkin. He made sure to keep a supply of the notepads on hand. Broom Stick even kept a stash behind the bar as a precaution. "What's his name, your brother?" Rick asked.

"Jon..." She stammered with practiced ease. "Jonathon Carlyle."

"Kidnapped or runaway?"

"I beg your pardon?"

"Did Jon--" He paused, much as she had, before continuing with his full name. "Did Jonathon run away from home?" He let the question hang in the air a beat before asking the all-important follow up. "Or did someone prompt his leaving? Was he in some kind of trouble?"

"I think it's safe to say that he ran of his own volition, Mr. Ruby."

"Tell me why," Rick said as Broom Stick silently dropped a fresh beer in front of him and removed his empty. Rick nodded his thanks, but never took his eyes off of Marilyn Carlyle.

"Back home," she started, before backtracking to add more details. "We're from California. Jonathon got himself in a little bit of trouble. I guess you could say he fell in with the wrong crowd. Thugs, I called them. I'm sure you know the type." Her eyes darted about the room as she spoke as if wondering how many thug types a dive joint like Belle's might attract.

If she only knew, Rick thought, but didn't speak it aloud. "I'm familiar with the type," he said instead, adding a playful chuckle, but did not elaborate further.

"Everything seemed fine until the week before last," she continued, her eyes once again focused on him. "Jonathon was frantic when he came by the house. He wanted money, said he had to get away for awhile, but he wouldn't tell me why or where he was going. I gave him what we had in the house, but he said it wasn't enough. I had never seen him so angry, Mr. Ruby. That was the last time I saw him."

"What makes you think he's here in New York?"

"He was always fascinated with the big city, New York in particular," she said with a short, dismissive laugh as if she couldn't believe anyone would choose the steel and concrete of The Big Apple over the sand and sun of California. "The glitz and glamour of the skyscrapers and the thrill of the constant hustle and bustle called to him. I think he would have moved here a long time ago if he had been able. Personally, I don't see the appeal."

"Different strokes," Rick said before taking another pull from his beer.

"He told me once that he was drawn to the romance of the city."

"This place has been known to have that effect on people," Rick said. It was true. Even a native New Yorker like himself still felt it from time to time. Despite all of the inhumanities he had seen on the job and even after his retirement, he still believed that New York City was truly the greatest city in the world. He couldn't understand why anyone would want to live anywhere else and he told her so.

"I hired a detective in California to track my brother down," she continued as if Rick hadn't spoken. "He was able to determine that Jonathon came here." She gestured her right hand in an all-encompassing circular motion, which he took to mean *here* as in *New York* as opposed to *here* meaning *Belle's*, although the way she said the word it was clear to Rick that she held both places in a similarly low regard.

"And since I don't know anyone in New York," she continued. "He suggested I hire a New York based private detective when I got here, someone who knew the lay of the land and had local contacts."

"I see," Rick said. "And that brought you to me."

"Not at first," she said, looking away as if embarrassed to admit that he wasn't her first choice. The pained look on her face told Rick that she wished she could take back the words. In an effort not to run off a potential paying client, he didn't press the issue as she covered with, "But that doesn't matter," she said. "I'm here now."

"That you are," Rick said with a slight thump of his palm on the bar top. He flashed her a professional smile that he reserved for clients who were less than honest with him, as he was certain she was being. He didn't know what she was lying about, but he was sure that she was being less than honest with him and he didn't like it. A part of him -the smart part- wanted to kick her to the curb because he knew he couldn't trust her, but another part -the one that often got him into trouble- that part was fascinated by this woman. It wasn't just her beauty, although he couldn't deny that she was a looker. He decided he would give her a little more rope and let the scenario play itself out. He just hoped she didn't hang herself before he could collect his fee.

"Do you have a photo of your brother?" Rick asked.

"Of course." She pulled a photo from her purse. It was a recent print as the edges were still squared off instead of worn like an older photograph would have been. As he studied the face two thoughts occurred to Rick. First was how unlike one another Marilyn and her brother looked, although that one could easily be explained as one favoring their mother while the other favored their father. Still, it was difficult to find so much as a mild resemblance. And second...

Well, he really didn't believe it. Something told Rick that Jonathon Carlyle wasn't really his new client's baby brother, but if she was lying about their relationship, he wasn't sure why. He still couldn't figure that part out and getting to the bottom of a good mystery always intrigued him. And his new client, whether she was a stone-faced liar or not, was definitely intriguing.

"Tell me about him," Rick told her, and listened as she laid out her story. By the time she finished, he still wasn't sure he could trust her, but he had decided to take the case.

✳ ✳ ✳

Rick Ruby met a lot of interesting people in his line of work.

Granted, most of them weren't exactly the kind of the folks he might ever want to meet in a dark alley, but he'd also discovered that even the meanest of bad guys had some quality about him that made him likeable. Some of the most entertaining poker games he'd ever been a part of had him sitting across the table from an ex-convict and former leg-breaker for the mob that had done time for murder. Rick didn't trust him any farther than he could throw him, but he did enjoy sharing beers and a smoke with the ex-con while taking his money at the poker table.

There were others. Much of the clientele, not to mention some of the staff, at Belle's had been on the wrong side of the law. Since he had turned in his badge and crossed that thin blue line, Rick had bent a law or two in order to solve a case. He didn't like it and in the early days as a P. I. it caused him some sleepless nights, but he eventually learned to live with it. The hard lesson he had to learn was that sometimes it was necessary to break the law in order to solve the case.

Drinking helped him cope with any moral dilemmas that cropped up. So did women.

One of Rick's regular stoolies was a blackout drunk named Dan Barrey. For all of his faults, and they were many, Dan had a conscience. Most of the time he tried to drown it with alcohol, but no matter how much he drank the voice of his conscience still came through loud and clear. Dan had a myriad of contacts with the local mobs as well as the local cons. He effortlessly walked both sides of the street without backlash because, for reasons no one could truly understand, everybody from the big boys from downtown to the local thugs liked Dan Barrey.

Rick had first met Dan back when he was a beat cop. He had offered Rick and his partner information on a hit that a local don was planning on one of their rivals. The hit was set to take place when the man picked his kid up from school one afternoon. Dan had gotten wind of it and quietly informed the cops. Dan didn't want to get in the middle of a shootout, but he also did not want anyone else to get hurt—especially not any kids—so he had told the Rick and his partner what he knew all in an effort to save innocent lives.

His information was rock solid and thus was a successful, if informal, partnership formed. Rick honestly liked Dan and had even tried to help him sober up a few times, but never with much success. Whatever demons were after him, Dan Barrey believed that the only help for him lay at the bottom of a bottle. Rick could sympathize. After those bastards had killed his girl, Greer, Rick spent six years chasing the same demon that Dan Bar-rey was still looking for. If not for his friend, Jack McGinnis, and a young girl named Beverly Terwilliger then he might still be searching.

Rick met Dan in the park the morning after taking the case. There was a nip in the air under a blanket of dark gray clouds that told him that fall would quickly turn to winter, which was a chilly proposition in New York. Dan, however, didn't appear to be in the mood for small talk so he kept his thoughts on the weather to himself. It was early and there was still frost on the ground. Rick wondered if Dan had slept in the park. It wouldn't have been the first time.

Dan coughed and raised a shaky hand to cover his mouth. "You sure you're okay?" Rick asked, not for the first time.

"I'm fine," Dan said as he wiped spittle on the frayed jacket he wore. "Damned sinuses are killing me."

"Right. Sinuses," Rick said, not believing his self-diagnosis.

Dan shot him a dirty look through bloodshot eyes. "I got a busy day ahead of me, Ruby. What do you want?"

Even after all the years they had known one another, Dan had never called him by his first name, which he found odd. Then again, Dan was an odd duck, so maybe it shouldn't have been so surprising. Early that morn-ing, Rick had taken his photo of Jonathon Carlyle to a camera shop and had duplicates made. Now he held one out. "You know this guy?" he asked.

"Should I?"

"He's new in town and apparently on the run," Rick explained. "If that's the case, he might be looking for a discreet place to hole up until the heat blows off him."

Dan took the photo and looked at it, squinting as he held it close to his eyes. Rick wondered why he didn't just take the pair of glasses off of his forehead and use them. He wanted to ask, but given his stoolie's mood he decided it was best to leave the matter be. "So what's your interest in him?" Dan asked.

"A woman claiming to be his sister hired me to find him?"

"Doesn't sound like you're all that convinced your client's on the up and up."

Rick grunted a soft laugh. "I'm not."

"Then why are you looking for this schlub?"

It was a good question, and one for which Rick really didn't have a good answer. "Her money's good," he said instead.

"So you're just going to find this guy and turn him over without know-ing the score?" Dan asked, eyeing the P. I. in a funny way. "That doesn't sound like you, Ruby."

Rick shuffled his feet, partly from the cold and partly because Dan knew him so well. "Well, let me find him first. Then I'll figure out what I'm going to do."

"Doesn't sound like much of a plan."

"It's the only one I've got," Rick said with a shrug. He pulled out a couple of bills from his wallet, folded them, then handed them over. "You think you could ask around for me?"

"I'll see what I can do," Dan said, pocketing both the money and the photograph. "You still got that cute secretary working for you?"

"Edie? Yeah, she still runs the office for me."

"Good," Dan said with a crooked smile. "Then I'll swing by your office later with whatever I can find on your lost sheep. Maybe I can even convince your Gal Friday to go out to dinner with me."

"Make sure you pick the place," Rick told him. "If you're not careful Edie'll have you down at the mission getting dried out."

Dan feigned a knife to the heart. "That sweet girl? Nah! She wouldn't dare!"

"You obviously don't know Edie Rose too well."

Dan blew out a breath.

"Okay," Rick said. "Don't say I didn't warn you. I appreciate the help, Dan. Is there anything else you need?"

"Nah," Dan said playfully. "I'm good, Ruby. You know me. All I need is a strong belt and I'm right as rain."

"So you keep telling me." Rick checked the time. "I've got to go," he said. "I'm meeting a friend over at the precinct."

"You're bringing the cops into this?"

"You aren't my only source of information, you know," he told Dan playfully.

"But the cops? Seriously?"

Rick smiled. "I used to be a cop, remember?"

"Lucky for me, you wised up," Dan said in a tone that Rick couldn't tell whether or not he was kidding.

"Tell that to my former captain," Rick joked. "I'll see you."

Dan Barrey turned and walked away, the sound of his coughing echoing off the brick walls of the surrounding buildings.

"You sure do like to live dangerously, Ruby," was the last thing Rick heard him say.

✳ ✳ ✳

It was snowing by the time Rick reached the precinct house.

He cursed aloud as he kicked the slush from his shoes just outside the entrance in a failed effort to keep from tracking water inside. One of the city's janitors was busy mopping up the water before someone slipped and fell. He didn't look any happier about the change in the weather than Rick.

Rick never knew what to feel when he strolled back inside the halls of the precinct he used to call home for five long years. On the one hand it felt like coming home, but on the other hand he was now an outsider. "When you're in, you're a guest. When you're out, you're a pest," he whispered as he made his way toward the detective's bullpen. He'd heard another former officer make the statement once, but had dismissed it at the time, but once he no longer held a badge he understood the sentiment all too well.

There were a few exceptions, though. Guys like Jack "Mac" McGinnis and Captain Franklin F. Connors were both good friends from his time working the beat, and they were still on good terms. After he pulled the pin and walked away from his pension and a shiny gold watch, these two men had helped him out on occasion, sometimes by thoughtfully tossing a little work Rick's way when he needed a little extra coin or a little information. Rick and Mac had once walked a beat together before moving up to the detective's desk. They remained the best of friends to this day. Captain Connors had been Rick's boss back in those days. He wasn't as close with the captain as he was with Mac, but it never hurt to stay on the good side of a police captain, especially for a P. I. Rick never knew when having friends in high places would come in handy.

Rick often repeated the mantra that "There's something to be said for having friends in high places."

Another good egg was William Blake. Blake was a rookie detective in the NYPD's robbery/homicide division so they had never worked together as cops, but a couple of their cases had crossed over and after Mac had vouched for him, they became buddies. He was still green enough that the other detectives had taken to calling him Billy Baby Face. Rick knew the young man hated the good-natured nickname, but he suffered in silence. Rick respected him for that. A couple of their cases had crossed paths, but after a rocky beginning, the two of them became pals. The kid had good instincts. Rick suspected he would go far in the department.

"Blake," Rick said as I entered the bullpen, drawing out the syllables.

"Well, well, well," the detective said as he rose from behind his battered steel desk to shake the P. I.'s hand. "What brings you all the way down to my neck of the woods in this miserable weather, Shylock?" He meant the nickname as a compliment and Rick took it as such.

"Where's Mac?"

Blake craned his head off to the left. "He's in with the captain. You know how these storms bring out the crazies."

"One part of the job I don't miss."

"I assume you're not here just to say howdy, so what can I do for ya?" Blake asked.

"I wanted to ask a favor," Rick told him as he took the chair he offered.

"I suppose I do owe you one after you helped us out with that nonsense over at Star Field last month," Blake said with a toothy grin. "What can I do for you?"

Rick fished out a photo of Jonathon Carlyle from a jacket pocket and passed it across the desk. "Missing persons case," he said. "A woman is looking for him and hired me to find him. She claims to be his sister."

"Claims to be?"

Rick shrugged his shoulders. "The jury's still out on that one."

"Missing persons really isn't my department, Rick." Blake leaned back in the padded metal desk chair and laced his fingers behind the back of his head. "I'd say it's probably more your realm of expertise than mine. What do you need me for?"

"Background. The guy's supposed to be from your old stomping grounds, California. I figured, who knows the West Coast better than you, right?"

"Ah," Blake said as he looked at the photo again. Billy Blake was born and raised in the Big Apple. When he was a teenager his family took John Soule's "*Go West, Young Man*" advice to heart and packed up and moved all the way out to the left coast to start a new life. Blake went from being an alley rat to a beach bum overnight.

The way he told the story, he surprised everyone when he applied to the police academy right after high school. Even more surprising to the family was that he got in. After spending a couple years working homicide in Hollywood division, Blake decided he missed the big city, packed a bag, and came back home. He'd been in New York ever since. That's been a good four... five years easily.

Blake still resembled the kid Rick first met years ago, mostly due to his boyish looks and the wad of chewing gum he continuously smacked on.

"California, huh? Well, there were some Carlyles suspected of having mob ties back when I was out in L.A., but I didn't know any of them personally. On one of the cases I worked back there we busted a mook named Victor Miles, supposedly a big wig in the family himself by all accounts."

"A woman is looking for him and hired me to find him."

"Sounds like you landed a whale."

"Something like that," Blake said, beaming with pride. It was the biggest bust he had made while working in California. He made his bones on that case only to come back to New York and be treated like a rookie all over again. "Once his operation came apart, a lot of the low-rung guys moved up in the organization. One of them was named Carlyle, but I don't remember if this guy was one of them off the top of my head, but I can do some digging, maybe make a couple calls."

"Thanks, Kid," Rick said, tossing his friend a nod. "I owe you one."

"No problem, Old Man," Blake replied with a grin as Rick walked away.

While William Blake consulted his contacts in California, Rick decided to try some good old-fashioned detective work.

Sometimes the tried and true methods were still the best way to solve a case. In this instance that meant thumbing through the phone book. If Carlyle was really on the run from the mob, one would assume he wasn't stupid enough to have his number listed. However, if there is one thing Rick had learned in his time as a cop and then as a private detective it's that criminals, despite whatever bloated opinion they might have of themselves, are not usually the brightest bulbs in the drawer. Even the smartest of the bunch always seemed to make one crucial mistake that would eventually lead to their downfall. If Carlyle fell into that category, Rick wondered what his fatal mistake would be.

And if this turned out to be true, Rick still had no idea what he was going to do about the client, who he was more convinced than ever was not who she claimed to be. But, his suspicious nature aside, there really wasn't much he could do about Marilyn Carlyle and her motives at the moment. *I'll jump off of that bridge when I get to it*, Rick decided.

First things first, he needed to find Jonathon Carlyle.

He would sort out the rest later.

There were several Carlyles listed in the yellow pages. No real surprise there. In a city the size of New York he would have been disappointed if there weren't. Of course, each of them would have to be called, which was not a task he was looking forward to, but a P. I.'s job was nowhere near as exciting as some of those radio dramas his friend Mac liked to listen to made them out to be. If asked, Rick would say that most of his cases were rather boring.

Rick sat in his office and dialed each number on the list in turn. With each answered call he asked a few pointed questions, sometimes pretending to work for the city, while others were more creative deceptions. It was boring work, but he had Edie Rose Adams, his secretary, keep the coffee coming while he worked. As enjoyable as a beer sounded at the moment, he made it a point not to drink when he was working. Or at least he tried to.

All of the phone numbers seemed on the up and up.

Except one.

Eighty-three-year-old Mavis Carlyle lived on the west side. After several unsuccessful attempts to reach her by phone, Rick decided to pay her a visit in person. A short, scary cab ride through the snowstorm later found Rick climbing the stairway to a lovely brownstone within in an easy walk from Central Park. Whoever Mavis Carlyle was, she sure did live high on the hog.

Rick knocked twice at the front door before deciding that no one was going to answer. He hoped that meant that elderly Mavis Carlyle wasn't home, but he'd been a cop too long to believe that. One of the perks of his current occupation, as opposed to his time as a police officer, was that he didn't require a search warrant or probable cause before entering a building. Of course, if he got caught, then the penalty for breaking and entering was quite severe. The last thing Rick's record needed was another B&E bust. The DA had been very adamant about that after the last time he got in trouble. He simply had to make sure he didn't get caught this time. Luckily, picking locks was a skill he had mastered very early in his career. Some locks were harder to crack than others, but the front door to Mavis Carlyle's home was not one of those. A fact for which he was thankful because his fingers had grown numb by the time he cracked the lock.

Rick smiled proudly as he pushed open the door.

The minute he stepped inside, he knew that something wasn't right.

There was no way a lady lived in this townhouse, no matter whether she was eighty-three or thirty-three. The apartment had the distinct feel of a bachelor pad. *Much like my own place*, Rick reminded myself. The question that he had to ask himself was *where was Mavis Carlyle?*

He kicked aside empty beer and soda bottles as he eased through the room. The smell of stale alcohol and sweat clung to every surface along with the unmistakable aroma of burnt dope. Rick's right hand tightened around the hilt of the slapper he kept in his coat pocket, a holdover from his days on the force. The slapper's weren't lethal, but anyone who took a hit from the small leather-encased weapon would think twice about getting back on his feet. "Building maintenance," he called out, just in case someone was at home.

There was no answer.

The hairs on the back of Rick's neck stood up on end. After so many years on the job, he could taste it in the air when something was wrong. It was a trait that all good detectives mastered over time. He eased through the open hallways and followed it. Three doors lined the hallways. The first was a bathroom, which was empty. He noted that the seat was up, further cementing his belief that no woman currently resided here. The second was a bedroom. It was empty, but had the feel of being a grandmother's room. From the amount of dust on the furniture, Rick guessed that it had lay empty for some time. The last door was ajar and he slowly pushed it open. Lying partway on a mattress on the floor was a man.

Rick immediately recognized Jonathon Carlyle from the photo his client had given him. Finding him had been far easier than he expected. If he had known it would be this easy he wouldn't have bothered Dan Barrey or William Blake about digging into it. Regardless, he would owe Dan a bottle of his favorite and Blake a steak dinner with all the fixin's.

Rick nudged the prone man and was relieved when he made a snorting sound. From the smell coming off of him, Jonathon Carlyle was sleeping one off in the spot where he'd dropped. He reeked of smoke and alcohol, plus he had apparently wet himself while passed out. Rick tried not to judge the man because he too had woken up more than once feeling less than his best as a result of the previous night's activities.

"Hey!" He nudged him again. "Jonathon! Can you hear me? Wake up!"

"Whu?" Carlyle's eyes snapped open as he was jolted awake. "Whuzzat?" he asked as he sat up on the mattress with his legs still outstretched before him. A hand went to his head, which was no doubt achy.

"Snap out of it," Rick said as he snapped his fingers in front of the boy's face. "Come on! Hey! Come on!"

"All right, all right," Jonathon Carlyle mumbled through dry, cracked lips as he rubbed his hands through the thick mop of hair that unruly pointed in multiple directions all at once. "Who the hell are you?" he finally asked once his eyes trained on the stranger standing in his bedroom.

"My name's Richard Ruby. Your sister, Marilyn, hired me to find you."

"My sister?" He scratched at the stubble on his chin, still not fully awake. "Marilyn? Marilyn hired you?"

"That's right," Rick said. "You sister is named Marilyn, right? A pretty blonde woman?"

"Yeah," he said softly. "Marilyn's my sister. Why is she looking for me?"

"She's worried about you," Rick explained. He had said her name purposely just in case his suspicions about his client were true, but maybe his gut had steered him wrong. It wouldn't be the first time.

"Well, congratulations, you found me," Jonathon said sarcastically. "So what happens now?"

"I guess that's up to you."

"What do you mean?"

Rick leaned against the doorjamb and crossed his arms over his chest. It was a maneuver he had used often as a cop because it usually reminded younger suspects of a disapproving parent. "Well, I'm obligated to tell my client that I found you. If you want to see her then I can help set that up in a neutral location and you two can catch up."

"Or?" Jonathon prompted.

"Or, if you tell me you don't want to see her then I can pass that message along, but I'd much rather go with the first option because, let's face it, you weren't hard to find."

"Alright," Jonathon said as he got to his feet. He was unsteady and smelled like the sewer grate in the alley behind Belle's on a busy night.

"Might I suggest a shower first," Rick offered.

Rick Ruby was happy.

As he usually did, Rick marked the successful completion of a case with a celebratory drink at Belle's. After he had gotten Jonathon Carlyle cleaned up and presentable, he called Edie Rose at the office and had her get in touch with the client and set up a meeting for later that afternoon. Rick chose to meet at Belle's since Marilyn wasn't from New York and she already knew how to get there. He figured that would be the easiest thing for her.

The reunion had gone fairly well. Jonathon Carlyle was still a bit bleary eyed when his sister arrived, but when she threw her arms around him he returned the embrace and smiled. Rick and Edie Rose sat at the end of the bar and watched the siblings as they moved over to a private booth where they talked for a solid half an hour.

After they had a chance to get reacquainted, Marilyn approached Rick and Edie, her high heels clicking as she walked. "I can't tell you how thrilled I am that you found him, Mr. Ruby," she said. "I am in your debt."

"Not for long, I hope," Rick said with a grin as Edie Rose handed Miss Carlyle an invoice for services rendered.

"Of course," she replied with a smile of her own. She opened the travel clutch she carried and pulled out the appropriate cash along with a little extra. "I'm including a small bonus for finding my baby brother so quickly," she said. "My family will be relieved to know that he is well."

"I'm just glad I could help," Rick said as he folded the money in half and handed it over to Edie Rose. She would see that it made it to the office instead of part of the pot of some poker game going on in the back room or stuffed in the corset of whichever one of Belle's performers had caught his eye that week.

Once the Carlyles left the bar—together, Rick noted—Broom Stick dropped a glass of top shelf bourbon on the bar in front of him. To his right, Edie Rose stood and collected her purse where she hid the money.

"Join me for a drink?" he asked her.

Edie Rose pursed her lips and shook her head. "I don't think so," she said, declining the invitation as she did every time he offered. In the time he had known her, Rick had only seen Edie Rose Adams drink once. By nature, she was demure and quiet, but there was a fiercely determined religious dynamo lurking beneath her tiny frame. Edie Rose was a sweet, kind person with a caring soul to match. She was probably the closest thing to family that Rick had, or would probably ever have.

"You sure?" he asked one more time, trying to tempt her to join him on the dark side. "Broom Stick mixes a mean one."

She smiled. "I'll see you in the morning, Rick."

Rick raised his glass in a toast as he watched her walk away.

Detective Jack "Mac" McGinnis hated the snow.

It wasn't the actual act of snowing or the fluffy white powder that bothered him. It was the way that the change in weather effected people. There was the contingent of New Yorkers who worried over being snowed in, so they ran to the nearest store to stock up on provisions just in case. He had been brought in to break up more than his fair share of fights inside a grocery store when the weather threatened snow. Then there were those who acted as though nothing had changed. It was these dummies who caused traffic accidents or fell on an icy patch. Of course, none of these compared to those poor few who went crazy.

Case in point, he and his partner, Detective William Blake, had been dispatched to investigate a phone tip about a body in an alley. It was just after dawn when Mac and Blake wrapped themselves up tight and ventured out into the blizzard that was only just beginning, if the weather reports were to be believed. Despite coats, gloves, hats, and scarves, both of them were shivering by the time they reached the alley in question.

One thing the snow did improve was the view. Even stacks of rotting garbage and other detritus could look pleasant under a blanket of winter weather. Mac and Blake walked carefully, sticking close to the walls so they had something to hold onto if one of them should slip. The last thing either of them needed was to fall and break something.

"Police," Mac called out. "Does anyone in the alley require assistance?"

No answer.

"I'm starting to think this is a wild goose, Mac. You want we should head back to the precinct where it's warm?"

"Not just yet, Kid. I think I see something," Mac said as he strained to see above a collective of overflowing garbage cans. "You there, behind the cans, can you hear me?"

No answer.

Mac walked forward, his right hand on the wall and his billy club in the left.

Blake stayed where he was, hand on his holster, just in case some lowlife was waiting for his partner. "What've you got, Mac?"

"It's clear," Mac said as he knelt next to something buried in the snow. With his gloved hands he cleared off the snow. "We've got a body," he called out to his partner, who hurried over to join him.

"He freeze to death?"

"I'd say probably not," Mac said as he pointed to the small caliber bullet hole in the center of the man's forehead. He wiped the snow off of the rest of the dead man's face, revealing day old stubble.

"Hey, wait a second," Blake said.

"What is it?"

"Mac, I know this guy."

"What?"

"Yeah. His name's Jonathon Carlyle."

Rick woke to the sound of pounding.

He wasn't sure if the obnoxious banging was coming from the door or from inside his screaming brain. Wherever the offended racket originated, it was as loud as it was painful. He rolled off the bed into a seated position and mentally vowed, as he had done so many times before, that he needed to stop drinking. He also realized that it was a hollow threat, especially with a bar full of free drinks at his disposal.

The banging resumed, but this time he recognized it as a loud knock at his door. "Yeah!" he shouted. "Hang on a minute!"

Another urgent round of knocks was his only reply. Whoever was out there was awfully impatient. Rick slouched across the room in his underwear. Before he could reach the door there was another loud knock.

"Hang on a minute, god--" he started.

Rick snatched open the door--

And was surprised to see Mac and Blake standing there.

"Geez! Finally," Mac said. "Where the hell have you been?"

"What's wrong?" Rick asked, his tone softer. He could only think of a handful of reasons why the guys might come knocking on his door at this early hour. None of them were good.

It was Blake that spoke up. "I found your missing brother."

"So did I," Rick said, the confusion evident on his face. "Yesterday. Didn't you get my message?"

Blake nodded.

"Wait," Rick said. "Where did you find him?"

"In an alley under a few inches of snow," Mac said.

"Was he high again?"

"No," Mac said. "He was dead."

※ ※ ※

"What do you mean, dead?"

That had been the first question Rick had asked, although in hindsight he realized that it was a pretty dumb thing to ask. As homicide detectives, Jack McGinnis and William Blake were quite familiar with dead bodies. After they had delivered him the news about the man that he had been hired to find, Mac and Blake gave him a ride to the morgue so he could positively identify the body of Jonathon Carlyle.

"Did you get in touch with his sister?" was the next thing he asked as he pulled on his clothes.

"We tried," Mac said.

"But it seems like no one knows where she is," Blake said, finishing his partner's thought. They had a habit of doing that and it annoyed Rick greatly, but he kept that insight to himself. "No one seems to have ever heard of her either, for that matter. Except you, of course."

"Now how is that possible?" Rick asked once they were on the move. "Not only did I check her credentials, but I even verified with the missing brother that she was his sister."

"What did the sister look like?" Blake asked from behind the wheel as he pulled out into the treacherously empty roads. The snow continued to fall as the temperature plummeted toward single digits.

Rick described her. "Tall and blonde. She was a looker, definitely comes from money or has gotten used to having it. A bombshell. You know the type."

"I talked to a friend of mine at the LAPD and he pulled a description on Jonathon Carlyle like you'd asked," Blake said. "Carlyle does have a sister named Marilyn, but she's only fourteen."

"The woman who hired me was definitely older than fourteen," Rick said. "Or they're growing up awfully fast out there in California."

"Sounds like you were set up, Rick," Mac said. "You got any idea where we can find this client of yours?"

Rick pulled the notebook from his shirt pocket, flipped it to the page where he had written down Marilyn Carlyle's contact information and passed it forward.

"This is a hotel, Rick." Mac's tone was accusatory, as if implying that his former partner should have known better.

"She told me she was in from out of town, Mac," Rick said through gritted teeth, trying to keep his anger in check. "Where else did you expect her to stay?"

"Good point."

"She was there when my secretary called her yesterday to tell her I found her brother. That much I know."

The hotel was between Rick's office and the morgue so they made a detour and stopped there first. Mac flashed his badge at the front desk and asked for Marilyn Carlyle's room, only to be told that she had checked out the night before and did not leave a forwarding address. There was also no home address on file since she'd paid in cash.

"Dead end," Mac told them once he was back at the car.

They continued on to the morgue where Rick gave a positive ID on Jonathon Carlyle's body. The bullet hole in the middle of his head looked so out of place that it made Rick sad. It didn't take long for sadness to turn to anger, however. From the size of the hole, he figured it was made by a .38. Mac and Blake agreed with his observation.

"This guy didn't deserve to die like this, Mac," Rick said after they left the cold concrete bunker that housed the morgue and stepped out into the cold Arctic chill of a New York winter.

"Nobody deserves to die like that," Mac replied.

"So what's our next move?" Blake asked.

"Simple," Rick said. "I'm going to track down Marilyn Carlyle, or whatever her name is, and she's going to explain to me exactly what the hell's going on. Even if I have to beat it out of her."

"I'm going to pretend I didn't hear you say that, Rick," Mac said. "For your sake."

"Yeah. Me too," Blake said.

"Thanks, guys," Rick said as he headed off to hail a cab back to his office. "I'll let you know when I find her."

For a private detective there was no worse feeling than being used by a client.

This wasn't the first time a client had lied to him. In fact, he figured he'd probably have a heart attack and die if one of his clients ever told him the whole truth without him having to pry it out of them. His experience with the woman claiming to be Marilyn Carlyle was the first time someone had lost their life as a result, however, and that did not sit well with Rick at all. A hard knot was forming in his gut at the thought of being used in such a manner.

To be fair, he had felt that something was off about the woman claiming to be Jonathon Carlyle's sister from the moment he first laid eyes on her at Belle's. He chose to ignore his gut because the boy seemed to go along with her deception, which in and of itself didn't make any sense. Why would he pretend that this woman was his sister if she clearly wasn't? He was in a place packed full of potential witnesses and Rick was there. All he had to do was say the word and Rick would have dealt with her right then and there, but he didn't and Rick couldn't understand why. He was safe. What did she have on him that would make Jonathon Carlyle support her lies and then leave with her? It didn't make sense. No matter how he tried to twist it, Rick couldn't come up with a plausible explanation and that frustrated him no end.

The only thing he knew for certain was that Marilyn Carlyle, his client, had betrayed him, and as a result of that betrayal a young man was dead.

Even though he knew it wasn't true, Rick felt responsible. He had led Marilyn, or whatever the hell her real name was, to Jonathon Carlyle and a few hours later he was dead. The more he replayed the timeline in his mind the madder he became.

So he decided to do something about it.

It was too late to help the boy, but he could still get justice for him. It was never too late for that. There was much to do so Rick headed back to his office.

There he found an unexpected surprise waiting for him.

Dan Barrey was obviously freezing as he stood outside in the winter weather. His frayed and ragged coat was cinched up tight, the collars lifted against the sides of his face in a futile effort to ward off the icy wind. A hand-rolled cigarette dangled from quivering lips, removed only long enough to take a swig from the bottle he had inside a brown paper bag.

"What are you doing out here?" Rick asked as he walked up to the stoop.

"Your girl up there wouldn't let me drink or smoke in your office, so I decided to wait for you out here?"

"Aren't you cold?"

"I was," Dan joked, shivering as he did so. "Now I'm too numb to feel it, so I guess I'm okay."

"Why are you here, Dan?"

"I found something for you, Ruby," he answered, staring at Rick as if he'd suddenly grown a second head. "You asked me to look into your missing beach boy, remember?"

"Right. Let's take this someplace a little warmer, huh? I'm freezing," Rick said as he plucked the tiny remnants of the cigarette from Dan's blue-tinged lips and tossed it into the snow bank before shepherding the man inside where it was warm.

"But your secretary--" Dan began to protest.

"You let me worry about that," Rick said. "Last thing I need on my conscience is you freezing to death on my stoop."

Rick led Dan upstairs to his office where he could feel the warmth of the office's stove. After his long walk from the precinct in the freezing cold it felt good to once again feel his fingers as sensation returned to them. Despite a disapproving look from Edie Rose, Rick ushered Dan into his office. "Can you get us some coffees?" Rick asked her before heading in behind his informant.

Edie Rose scowled, but complied.

Rick draped his coat over the back of his chair and took a seat in it behind his desk near the window and opened the bottom drawer where he kept his gun. "What have you got for me, Dan?" he asked as he put the gun on his desk along with a wire brush.

"You remember that guy you asked me to track down?"

"Yeah."

"Well, I tracked him down."

"So did I."

"Really?" Dan's mood darkened. "I still get paid, right?"

"Of course, Dan," Rick said as he loaded the pistol. "Tell me what you have, but just stick to the important details. I'm in a bit of a hurry."

"I can tell," Dan said, his eyes locked on the gun Rick was loading. "I found out that guy you were looking for wasn't just missing, he was hiding."

"Hiding from whom?"

"Your boy got himself into a tight spot. The way I hear it, Jonathon Carlyle never met a wager he didn't like. Unfortunately, the feeling wasn't mutual. Plus, he also liked the dope a little too much and that didn't make for a smart gambler. He was in hock big time."

Rick blew out a breath and shook his head, mentally chastising himself for not seeing it himself. "Anybody I know?"

"He owed several of the usual suspects, but the bulk of his debt was to the Derek Shaunessey."

"Great," Rick muttered. "The Irish Mob."

"That's the one," Dan said, happy that his information had been needed after all.

"How the hell did this kid get mixed up with those thugs?"

"Beat's me," Dan said. "You think maybe your client works for Shaunessey?"

"I wouldn't be surprised."

Rick stood and slipped on a shoulder holster. He holstered the pistol then slipped back on his coat. "Thanks for the info, Dan. It was a big help."

Dan stood, concern lining his features. "You aren't planning on taking on Shaunessey by yourself, are you? Stunts like that'll get you killed, Ruby."

"Rick stood and slipped on a shoulder holster."

Rick slapped him on the shoulder. "I appreciate the concern, Dan, but don't worry, I've done this sort of thing before."

"Committing suicide is something most folks only do once, Ruby."

Rick turned around and clucked his teeth. "Why don't you hang out here for the night, Dan. The couch ain't much, but it's comfortable enough."

"I don't need no charity, Ruby. Just give me the money I earned and I'll make my own accommodations."

Rick moved in close and dropped his voice to just above a whisper. "Consider this another job," he said. "If he knows I'm on to him, Shaunessey might send someone here looking for me." He turned to look at Edie Rose behind her desk, pretending not to eavesdrop. "I'd hate for Edie Rose to be here all by herself if that happens," he said, knowing that his secretary kept a loaded gun in her desk and another in her purse. She could take care of herself.

"Fine," Dan said.

"Thanks, buddy," Rick said as he walked out of the office. "I owe you one."

"Just remember," Dan said behind him. "Dead men can't pay their debts, Ruby."

Rick had crossed paths with Derek Shaunessey before.

It had been a few years since they had last met, back when Rick was still carrying a badge, but Rick remembered the "self-made businessman" all too well. Rick Ruby was not a man that held on to many regrets, but of the few he could never quite let go of, Derek Shaunessey was near the top of the list.

Shaunessey had an office on the top floor of one of New York's newest and tallest skyscrapers. Rick thought the building suited the criminal since he thought he was god-like above the little people he stepped over to get what he wanted. He though he was untouchable.

Rick planned to show him the error of such hubris.

As he approached the Essey Tower building, home of Shaunessey Enterprises, Rick noticed that the heavily muscled doorman was strapped, a gun tucked at each side, held in place by a shoulder holster he couldn't see. The doorman stepped forward at his approach, positioning himself between the angry P. I. and the entrance.

"Step aside, King Kong," Rick told the doorman as he took the steps two at a time, thankful that they had been cleared of snow and ice and salted. He was a bruiser, who stood a couple inches taller than he, plus Rick was a few steps down from the entrance. The thug at the door towered over him.

"You'd better just turn around and go back where you came from," the doorman said. His voice was deep and heavily accented.

"Not until I see your boss," Rick said matter of fact.

"Don't say I didn't warn you," the doorman said as he reached for him.

Still two steps away from the landing in front of the door, Rick shifted, grabbing the doorman by his beefy arm and twisted, pulling the bruiser forward and throwing him off balance. The doorman's own momentum took care of the rest. Rick released him and watched as he bounced down the steps and came to rest near a snow bank on the sidewalk.

Rick didn't waste any time gloating. Instead, he turned on his heel and pushed his was through the glass doors into the lobby. He was already two steps inside before Kong's back up stepped out of a hidden security alcove and intercepted him. "Hold it right there, sir," the man told Rick. Like his friend outside, this one was a big bruiser as well. Rick smelled the unmistakable twinge of whiskey combined with cigarette smoke. It was not the first time he'd encounter that aroma.

"Tell your boss that Richard Ruby's here to see him. He knows me," Rick said, his anger threatening to boil over. "Or do you want to join your friend out there?" He cocked his head in the direction of the main door where the banged up doorman was cautiously climbing back up the stairs while holding his left arm, which had clearly broken in the fall. A subtle shake of the head from the security guard brought him up short and he held his position outside.

The security guard gritted his teeth as he studied the rumpled P. I. Rick assumed he was debating whether or not to try his luck. In a fair fight, Rick knew that the guard would take him every time, but Rick had an ace in the hold. He smiled as his fingered the brass knuckles in his coat pocket. He wasn't planning on a fair fight.

"Well?"

"Just a moment," the guard said as he nodded to another man, this one a bit more wiry. He worked the desk. Rick watched him dial a number and wait. He spoke so quietly into the phone that Rick couldn't hear what he was saying, but he could guess what they were discussing. After a moment, the wiry guy hung up then made his way over to the security guard. Same as with the phone call, Rick couldn't hear what was being said, but there were really only a handful of possible outcomes. They would either escort him upstairs to see the boss, they would toss him out on his ear, or they might just put a bullet between his eyes and dump him out back. The last option seemed a bit farfetched considering all of the efforts Derek Shaunessey had been putting into making himself appear to be a legitimate businessman.

"Mr. Shaunessey will see you," the security guard said, but he didn't look happy about it. "Before I let you up there I'm going to have to search you and confiscate any weapons."

Rick raised his arms, exposing the holster and pistol. The guard took it and, after a quick pat down, took the brass knuckled and the knife Rick had concealed in his boot. "I'm going to want those back," Rick said as the guard set them on the desk and motioned him toward the bank of elevators. "They were a Christmas present from a friend."

No one laughed at the joke. Instead, Rick and the security guard waited silently on the elevator. Once the lift arrived, they rode toward the penthouse without speaking, although Rick couldn't resist the urge to whistle a short little ditty as the car shimmied its way up the shaft.

Once the elevator lurched to a stop, Rick stepped out into the private outer office. Expensive art adorned the walls, interspersed with potted plants and imported rugs. Behind the receptionist's desk sat a stunningly beautiful woman who would have been right at home on a pin-up calendar. On the wall behind her was a large lighted sign with Shaunessey Enterprises is raised type, back lit against a dark green background that played up the owner's Irish heritage.

"Welcome to Shaunessey Enterprises, Mr. Ruby," the receptionist said around a big, toothy smile. Her voice was as sweet as honey. "Mr. Shaunessey is expecting you." She motioned toward the closed door that led to the boss's office. "Please, go on inside."

Rick accepted the invitation with only a nod toward the secretary. The main office was much more polished than the exterior one. Even more expensive art framed two of the walls along with a couple marble statues that looked like they belonged in a museum instead of on display in a private office. A couch and two chairs surrounded a small coffee table in a corner and another chair was near the desk. Its lone occupant was a brunette woman whose face Rick couldn't see. As if he were not worth her attention, the woman did not turn as he entered. Instead, she stared out the window, a drink in one hand and a freshly lit cigarette in the other. Through the slit of her dress he noticed her shapely stocking-covered legs, one draped over the other casually.

The other two walls of the office were made up entirely of windows with a sweeping view of New York City spread out below him. Shaunessey's desk sat angled between the windows, the corners of the office meeting directly behind his chair. The man himself stood in the corner, hands draped behind his back, staring down on the city.

From the moment he stepped inside, Rick knew what this office represented.

Power.

Derek Shaunessey had it and he knew how to flaunt it.

"Mr. Ruby," he said without turning around to look at his visitor, a thick cigar clenched between two fingers. "I understand you wish to speak with me. My staff tells me that you were most..." He turned around and flashed the P. I. with a predatory smile before continuing. "Insistent."

Rick chuckled as he took a step forward. "Well, in my line of work, it's the squeaky wheel that gets the grease, as they say." He sensed the security guard stiffen behind him, but a nod from Shaunessey kept him at bay. He wouldn't take any action until he knew the P. I.'s intentions.

"I often find that the best way to deal with a squeaky wheel is to have it greased," Shaunessey said, the predatory smile still in place, the threat hard to miss.

Rick chose to ignore it and pressed on. "I know it's been awhile, but you still don't intimidate me."

A cloud of confusion crossed Shaunessey's face. He tried to hide it by quickly putting the cigar back in his mouth, but Rick noticed. "I thought you looked familiar. It's Detective Ruby, isn't it?"

Rick chuckled. "Not for a while now," he said. "I'm more of an independent contractor these days."

"A private dick, eh?" Shaunessey said playfully as he motioned for Rick to take a chair even as he pulled out his own desk chair. "Who would have thought it? One of New York's finest finally decided to step over to the dark side of the street. How you like playing in my sandbox, Mr. Ruby?"

Rick sat in the offered chair and crossed one leg over the other. He looked comfortable. "It's..." he paused as if searching for just the right word. "Freeing," he finally said.

"How so?"

"Well, let's just say that without those pesky laws getting in the way I'm able to bypass the red tape that used to keep me from breaking some bum's nose when the situation warranted." He smiled across the polished wood desk. Shaunessey wasn't the only one capable of making veiled threats.

Rick could intimidate with the best of them with or without a badge.

Shaunessey leaned forward, elbows on the desk, dark gray smoke curling around his thick face. "So what is it I can do for you?" he asked.

"Simple," Rick said, still looking as comfortable as a man sitting in his own living room. "I want you to tell me who murdered Jonathan Carlyle."

"I beg your pardon?"

Out of the corner of his eye, Rick saw the brunette flinch, confirming his suspicions. "You heard me," he said as he returned his full attention back to the gangster.

"I'm afraid I don't follow you. Who is Jonathan Carlyle and what makes you think I know who killed him?"

Rick smiled. "Let's just call it a hunch, shall we?"

Shaunessey stood and pushed back his chair. "I think it's time for you to leave," he said.

Rick got to his feet slowly. "Fine. I'll go," he said, but then leaned in closer to the desk and dropped his voice to just above a whisper. "But I'm not going far."

Just then the outer door opened and the big, beefy security guard entered. He did not look happy. "Mr. Ruby is ready to go," Shaunessey told him.

"Yes, sir."

As he was being escorted toward the door, Rick cast a final glance at the brunette staring out the window. "Catch you later, Marilyn," he said, playing his last card.

The brunette jerked as if startled, which confirmed Rick's suspicions. Marilyn Carlyle or whatever her name was, his client, was a stone-cold killer. She and her boss had played him for a sucker and now a man was dead as a result. Rick could not let that stand. Derek Shaunessey thought he was untouchable in his ivory tower overlooking his interests. He had built a vast and mighty empire.

Rick Ruby was going to bring the whole thing crashing down around his ears.

Rick Ruby was angry.

Guys like Derek Shaunessey were used to getting their way. But he'd made a fatal mistake this time. Rick was not a man who took threats very lightly. Plus, he knew how to defend himself. He stopped at the nearest payphone, wiped away the snow with a gloved hand, then dropped in a dime before dialing his own number. Edie Rose Adams answered on the second ring. "I need you to do something for me and don't ask any questions," he told her.

After finishing up with Edie Rose, Rick made a second call, this one to Jack McGinnis at his old police precinct. He filled in Mac on what had happened inside Shaunessey's penthouse office and, after receiving an earful from his friend about the recklessness of going there alone, told him what he was thinking. Mac listened quietly, not interrupting as Rick laid out his plan. Mac wasn't thrilled, but he agreed to back up his former partner.

By the time he returned to his office, it was empty. For once, Edie Rose had actually done as she was told and gone home. He was surprised. He loved her like a little sister and she annoyed him in that way that only family could. When Derek Shaunessey came for him - and Rick had no doubt that trouble was coming - he wanted Edie Rose as far out of the line of fire as possible.

After adjusting the office door just right so that it hid his back up plan, Rick called down to the bar and gave Broom Stick a heads up just in case Shaunessey's hired gun took a wrong turn in the stairwell. Broom Stick asked if Rick needed any back up, but he declined and told him it was being taken care of. He did ask Broom Stick to keep an eye on Belle and her girls, just in case.

With all of the players in place, Rick poured himself a couple of fingers of bourbon from the expensive bottle he kept in the bottom drawer of his desk and downed it in one shot. After walking in the icy conditions outside, the burn of the alcohol felt good. He shrugged off his coat and hung it on the rack in the corner. He set the gun on the desk within arm's easy reach. With the only light in the room coming through the blinds over the lone window stenciled with Richard Ruby, Private Investigations, he sat back in his desk chair and poured himself another drink, this time filling the cup. He leaned back comfortably, propped up his feet, and sipped at the smooth bourbon.

"And now we wait," he said into the darkness.

He didn't have to wait long.

The first thing he recognized was her scent. It was the same unmistakably sweet floral smell that she wore when last they met. Only this time Rick did not find it as alluring as he did then. Seconds later he heard the familiar *clack, clack, clack* of high heels on the stairs outside the office.

He sat the glass down on the desk and crossed his right leg over the left comfortably, his right hand resting on the desk near his gun, but made no move to get to his feet.

The outer office door opened and he watched as his not unexpected guest eased around the frame. She was trying very hard to sneak in un-detected and he hated to disappoint her so he sat in silence so as not to disturb her. Despite the job that she was there to carry out, Rick couldn't help but be impressed with her skill at breaking and entering.

"Hello, Marilyn," he said, shattering the silence. "I've been waiting for you."

She froze.

"You can cut the act, sister. I know you're there."

"Am I supposed to be impressed?"

Rick laughed as he watched her walk toward his office door. Only her legs were clearly defined as she walked through a shaft of moonlight through the window. "Not at all," he said matter of fact. "You were ex-pected."

She clucked her teeth.

"That's close enough," Rick said as he pulled the chain on the small desk lamp with the shade tilted away from him so it would shine directly in her eyes without blinding him as well. The light poured away from him and shone a spotlight on the woman whom he knew only as Marilyn Carlyle.

She stopped and spread her arms wide as if in surrender.

He didn't buy it for a minute.

As before, she was dressed to kill, this time more literally than before. She wore black pants stretched firmly over her muscular legs with high heels. An equally tight black sweater completed the ensemble. The only ac-cessory out of place was the .38 she held in her manicured hand.

"Lose the gun," Rick ordered.

Marilyn's ruby red lips parted in a toothy smile. Under different cir-cumstances, it was a smile that could melt Rick's wounded heart. Now he found it terrifying. "You hardly seem in a position to give orders," she said, her eyes focusing on his gun, which lay on the desk. "Or do you really think you're that fast?"

"Probably not," Rick chuckled. "Thankfully, I don't have to be."

"What're you..." Before she could say more, Marilyn turned her head toward the small creaking sound that was the office door moving. She was already turning when she heard an all too familiar clicking noise and felt the cold muzzle of a gun press against the side of her head.

"Ah, ah, ah," Mac McGinnis said as he stepped from his hiding place behind the office door. He plucked the weapon from her hand. "I'll take that, thank you."

Marilyn sighed, but otherwise seemed undisturbed by her imminent arrest.

"Now, there's two ways this can go down," Rick said as he rose from his desk chair. "My friend here can take you downtown and book you on suspicion of murder--"

"Which I'm fairly sure I can make stick now that I've got this," Mac said, shaking her gun in his fist.

"Or," Rick continued as he walked closer. "Or you can spill the beans on Derek Shaunessey's business. Then we'll see what kind of deal we can cut for you."

Marilyn laughed. "That's not much of a deal."

"It's the best one you're going to get, sister," Mac said.

Marilyn looked at Mac, her smile gone. "Perhaps you would like to hear a counterproposal?"

"This should be good," Rick said with a smirk.

She smiled and Rick realized, too late, that she had not come alone.

That's when the window behind Rick exploded.

Rick's ears were ringing.

Disoriented, he pushed himself up from the floor, not quite sure how he'd even gotten there in the first place. Everything sounded garbled and fuzzy, as if his ears had been packed with cotton. The only sound that came through loud and clear was as excruciatingly painful whistling noise.

He lifted his head and instantly regretted it as pain shot out from behind his eyes, causing his vision to blur in and out of focus. Rick dropped back to the floor, but he could see two people nearby. One of them he recognized with ease.

"Mac?" he shouted, but his friend didn't stir. He was face down on the rug near the entrance to his inner office, the door wide open. Lying partway beneath his former partner was a woman. From the looks of it, Mac had thrown her to the ground and covered her with his own body as a makeshift shield.

He remembered the woman and events came flooding back to him. On all fours, Rick crawled over to check on Mac. He was unconscious, but at least he was alive. Blood poured from a wound on his left arm. Someone had shot him.

Rick tore a strip from his sleeve and tied it around Mac's arm, stanching the flow of blood. It was a temporary measure at best. Mac would need a doctor, but Rick had a sneaking feeling that whoever had shot at them from across the street would arrive soon enough to make sure the job was finished.

He took Mac's handcuffs and put one around Marilyn Carlyle's arm and fastened the other end around the radiator on the wall near the door. He slid Mac away from the open door as well. Rick wanted to prepare a special little surprise for the man coming, but he had to act quickly before it was--

Too late!

The outer officer door opened violently as it was pushed inward by a kick from a heavy boot. A big man stepped into the darkened office, a high caliber rifle in his hand. Rick immediately recognized Derek Shaunessey. He was both surprised and a little impressed that the boss man was dealing with this personally.

Instinctively, Rick's hand went for his gun, but the holster was empty. That's when he remembered that he had set the gun on his desk. There was no way to reach it before Shaunessey saw him.

Think, Rick, think! Moving on instinct, Rick kicked the door to his inner office closed. Before it could even slam shut he was moving. He grabbed his gun and dove behind his desk seconds before a second volley of gunfire tore through the wall.

Rick pressed himself as far into the floor as he could while hot lead ripped his office to shreds. For all the trouble he'd had getting that heavy oak desk into his office, he was thankful for it. Splinters were flying all over the office like tiny missiles, but the desk remained more or less intact against the onslaught.

The bullets stopped and Rick let out a breath. Whatever else he might be, Derek Shaunessey was a thug. He knew how to handle a weapon, as the remnants of Rick's office could attest. Shaunessey was also a prideful S.O.B. Rick had purposefully pushed his buttons when they met in his fancy over-decorated office. He wanted to provoke a reaction, get the gangster to make a mistake and tip his hand.

Well, Ricky boy, he told himself. *You asked for it. You got it. Now what are you going to do with it?*

Rick kept his head down, but stayed focused on the door, only occasionally casting a glance in Mac's direction to make sure he was okay. He was still out like a light, but otherwise hadn't sustained any new injuries in the last attack. Marilyn, or whatever her name was, similarly slumbered near him.

The sound of glass and wood crunching beneath heavy boots echoed through the room as Derek Shaunessey approached the office. Rick cocked the pistol slowly, trying to stay as silent as possible. If Shaunessey thought he had missed then he would simply open fire again until the desk was destroyed or he got in a lucky strike. Rick leaned on the edge of the desk and supported his aim by lying his arms on the top while he stood in a crouch. As disoriented as he felt he had to make the first shot count. He knew it was quite possible he wouldn't get a second.

When Derek Shaunessey stepped through that door he was in for one hell of a surprise.

As he did with the outer office door, Shaunessey kicked open the office door with a powerful swing. He stepped one foot inside the office and swept the room, leading with the rifle. When his gaze fell on Rick Ruby leaning on the desk it took him a second to process that he wasn't lying there dying.

He was waiting for him.

"Missed me," Rick said without humor.

Shaunessey started to speak, but he was too late.

Rick pulled the trigger twice.

The sound was deafening.

The muzzle flash lit up the room, casting odd shadows through the haze and dust hanging in the air. Everything moved in slow motion as Rick watched the bullet tear into Derek Shaunessey's shoulder, the impact spinning him back toward the door, but not dropping him to the floor. The rifle flew from his hand and clattered to the floor.

Rick made his move just as time resumed its normal flow. Moving purely on instinct and adrenaline, he launched himself from the desk toward the gangster, slamming into him. Together, they hit the door, breaking what remained of the glass and shattering the thin wood. Rick angled himself to land atop the would-be assassin when they crashed to the floor. Still dizzy from the attack, Rick pressed the advantage, landing blow after blow on the gangster before he could recover. Shaunessey easily had one hundred and fifty pounds on the battered P. I., which made this the closest thing to a fair fight Rick was liable to get.

Shaunessey countered with a left hook that caught his opponent under the chin. Rick felt teeth rattle and saw stars when he bit his tongue. He fell backward and slammed into his secretary's desk, which, like his own was all but destroyed. The thought of having to go out shopping for replacement furniture with Edie Rose barely had time to form before the gangster was on him again.

For a big guy, Derek Shaunessey was fast. A left hook knocked Rick to the floor. He rolled out of the way before a second punch was landed. He kicked out with his left leg and heard bone crunch, quickly followed by the big man's scream. Rick pressed the advantage and put everything he had into a haymaker.

The punch landed with a resounding THUMP, and Derek Shaunessey dropped to the floor in a heap.

Rick followed suit and collapsed to the floor, spent.

He wasn't sure how long he lay there.

It could have been minutes or hours, Rick really wasn't sure. One moment he was alone in the office, the next Mac was shaking him to make sure he was all right. "Glad to see you're still with us, pally," Mac said with a smile.

"You okay?" Rick asked as he pointed toward the bloodstains on his friend's shirt. It took all of his energy to raise his arm for the gesture.

Mac smiled. "Just a scratch," he said.

"Yeah, right," Blake said from nearby. He had arrived with the back up just like they'd planned.

"Did you get 'em all, kid?" Rick asked as he got to his feet with Blake's help.

"Oh yeah. Shaunessey brought plenty of help. We got all of them while they were waiting outside. Apparently, the big man didn't like you too much, Rick. They said he wanted to take care of you personally."

"I guess I should be honored," Rick said without humor.

Rick leaned against the broken desk and watched as the uniformed officers escorted Derek Shaunessey and the woman that he knew only as Marilyn Carlyle out of the office in handcuffs. A paddy wagon was waiting downstairs to escort them all to the precinct house for booking along with a dozen armed officers as backup just in case any of Shaunessey's gangster friends decided to ambush them en route to the station and spring their boss.

"I'll need you to come downtown and make an official statement too," Blake said. "Both of you."

"You got it, Kid," Rick said as he rubbed the back of his sore neck. "I could really use some shut eye," Rick told Mac once the criminals were carted out of the office.

"I could use a drink," Mac said.

Rick perked up and smiled. "I like your idea better."

"I thought you might."

"I know just the place," Rick said as he clapped his friend on the back as they walked out of the office.

"Why am I not surprised?"

Rick turned to look back into the office. It was all but destroyed. "I do have just one question though."

"What's that?" Mac asked.

"Who's going to clean this mess up?"

The End

IT'S ALL SEAN TAYLOR'S FAULT
THE BIRTH OF THE RUBY FILES

It's all Sean Taylor's fault.

Sean and I, like many other Airship 27 writers, are members of an online group called The Pulp Factory. We quite often have spirited discussions about all things pulp at the Pulp Factory, and one day the discussion turned toward pulp private investigators. There was a lot of back and forth debating what makes a good pulp P. I. And going through examples of the hardboiled private eyes from the old pulps, TV, and movies. It was a great discussion.

Did I mention that it was all Sean Taylor's fault?

It isn't often that I step away from the internet for long periods of time, but on this particular December day in 2010 I was busy doing something that kept me away from the computer all day. When I finally checked my email, I saw all of the posts about pulp P. I.s and started reading through them. At one point it was mentioned that Airship 27 should create a hardboiled P. I. anthology as part of their pulp anthology line. I thought it was a good idea, but since my plate was pretty full I really didn't give it much more thought until I hit a post by Sean Taylor.

Seriously, it's all Sean Taylor's fault.

For those who might not know Sean, and if that's you then you should really check out his work, there's even a story by him in this very volume so you won't have to look too hard. But I digress. Where was I again? Oh, yeah. Sean, in addition to being a heckuva writer, is a friend of mine. We often travel to conventions together. So, anyway, I read Sean's post wherein he mentioned possibly creating a new pulp P. I. character and mentioned my name. Sean and I had pitched an idea to another publisher a couple years earlier about reviving a pulp TV detective, but nothing ever happened, so this was a good way to tell those same type of stories.

At that point, Ron Fortier, our editor, the smart man that he is, said it sounded like a great idea and that we, Sean and I, should put together a series bible. As we were coming up on Christmas, we decided to meet up after the first of the year after we each finished up our stories for *Lance Star: Sky Ranger Volume 3* (shameless plug). Sean and I were both guests on the Earth Station One podcast that was recording live at a comic book shop so we headed out to dinner afterward to hammer out the genesis of what would become Rick Ruby, pulp private eye.

I still fondly recall the three of us (Sean, his daughter, Charis, and me) sitting in the restaurant as the people seated near us were eavesdropping on our spirited discussion that included guns, booze, dangerous dames, jazz, brass knuckles, and mobsters. Lord only knows what they thought we were up to over a good meal.

So, as I mentioned earlier, it really is Sean Taylor's fault.

If not for Sean mentioning the idea of creating a pulp P.I., the volume you hold in your hand might not exist and that would be a shame. The writers in this volume have crafted some incredible pulp tales and I'm proud to be one of the co-creators of The Ruby Files. I hope we'll be reading Rick's adventures for many years to come.

So, yeah, it was all Sean Taylor's fault.

BOBBY NASH - Writes from his secret lair in the wilds of Bethlehem, Georgia. A multitasker, Bobby's certain that he does not suffer from ADD, but instead he... *ooh, shiny.* When he finally manages to put fingers to the keyboard, Bobby writes novels (*Evil Ways, Fantastix*), comic books (*Fuzzy Bunnies From Hell, Demonslayer*), short prose (*A Fistful of Legends, Full Throttle Space Tales Vol. 2: Space Sirens, Green Hornet Case Files*), novellas (*Lance Star: Sky Ranger, Ravenwood: Stepson of Mystery*), graphic novels (*Yin Yang, I Am Googol: The Great Invasion*), and even a little pulp fiction (*Domino Lady, Secret Agent X*) just for good measure. Despite what his brother says, Bobby is not addicted to buying DVD box sets and can quit anytime he wants to.

You can check out Bobby's work at www.bobbynash.com, www.lance-star.com, www.facebook.com/bobbyenash, and www.twitter.com/bobby-nash, among other places across the web.

TULSA BLACKIE'S LAST DIVE
By William Patrick Maynard

Jasmine…he could smell Jasmine in the air as he looked up at the stars glittering in the night sky. The toughest part about acting for the cameras was when there was no dialogue or action…like now. He could get his tongue around the two-bit dialogue J. C. wrote and he could handle himself well enough with his fists, jump on a horse, ride and take a tumble like the best of them, but standing still or walking took concentration. At times like this he had to imagine the smell of Jasmine and let it carry him through the scene. He would glide like the wind.

He was gliding now as he undid the tassel of his monogrammed terrycloth bathrobe. His shoulders slumped as he let the robe slip effortlessly down his back and crumple at his feet. He stood there buck naked smelling that Jasmine. The stars were bright tonight, but not as bright as the heat from the arc lamps. He could feel them sizzling down on his spine. He was a big man, muscular with great dense limbs and a barrel chest. His width made him look far taller than his 5 feet, 9 inches.

Best ass in Hollywood, wasn't that what they called him? There might have been a joke there, but he didn't care so long as the money was green and plentiful. It didn't matter how corny the scripts were or that he was stuck at a rundown studio instead of with one of the majors. He had been with Fox for awhile, it was no big thing. Of course, he was only doubling for that song and dance feller, but still at least now he was a star even if it was in a little pond.

Tulsa Blackie, hero of every boy between the ages of three and nine. Once they got to the double digits, they yearned to see something more sophisticated than Tulsa Blackie riding ol' Buck, but he didn't give a damn what anybody thought of him. He was just like Ma. Ma didn't care one whit what folks thought of her when she left his Pappy and all that oil money to come to Hollywood. Things didn't work out like she planned, but she got by. He was just like Ma.

He stumbled on his feet a bit. That Jasmine was intoxicating tonight! Good thing there weren't any cameras about or that damn fool director would be yelling cut and cussing at him for ruining the take. Of course there weren't any picture theaters that would show a picture with Tulsa Blackie prancing around naked as a baby like he was tonight. Back at the studio, the Old Man might run that sort of picture during his gin parties, but no respectable theaters would show them.

Steady now, boy, don't fall off that diving board, not unless you want to make that director mad.

What director? He shook his head to clear his mind of the Jasmine. It was getting so he couldn't remember which end was up. Well, a nice refreshing swim would clear his perspective. That was just the thing he needed.

He stretched his arms toward the ceiling and felt his back arch. This would look great if only the cameras were there to capture it. He was acting natural for a change and not going through third-rate paces like J. C.'s scripts demanded. He took a deep breath hungry for that soothing water to get the scent of the Jasmine out of his nostrils and throat. It was so thick he felt like choking.

Steady now, boy, you're almost there.

He trotted forward, surprisingly nimble for a man his size and dove straight up and then down. The water was so close he could almost taste it.

There was no splash. Tulsa Blackie's last dive ended in a skull-shattering impact with the marble floor of his penthouse apartment's empty swimming pool. Crazy red patterns spread wet and wild all over the floor and ran up the sides before sliding back down in a dizzying cascade of color. Maybe the newspaper men would say it was the mark of a true artist. Ma would have been proud.

The applause was always guaranteed to bring a smile to the performer's face.

"Thank you very much. Next I'd like to do a new number from Cole Porter. This one is called 'Easy to Love.' This one is for my special someone and maybe that's you."

Evelyn had them eating out of her hands tonight and Rick felt a swelling in his right pocket as he considered she might very well be talking about him. He put his hands behind his head and stretched back in his chair. The smile that split his face like a jack-o'-lantern made him look like an innocent kid without a care in the world.

That was about to change.

"Mr. Ruby."

It wasn't a question so much as a statement.

Rick looked back at the thin, hawk-faced bespectacled suit standing next to his table with both hands clasping a battered leather briefcase. He took in the coat and the hat and figured them for only about ten years old. Not bad for anybody these days.

"Something I can do for you, friend?"

The suit pulled the chair back and placing the briefcase before him on the table, he sat stiffly next to Rick.

"My name is Carl Obermeier…or Junior to most people. I'm with Monorail Pictures."

Rick leaned his chair forward and steadied himself with his palms flat on the table.

"Oh sure, the son also rises. Monorail Pictures, how does that slogan go?"

"If it's a quickie, it must be Monorail."

Obermeier's voice betrayed no emotion whatsoever as he repeated the phrase his father had coined to appear with their logo at the start of every Monorail production.

"I'm as partial to a quickie as the next fellow," Rick laughed amiably as he leaned forward, "but to be perfectly honest with you, Mr. Obermeier, I'm enjoying a little vacation starting tonight. You see, I've had a run of rare good luck and I'm planning on enjoying every last dime of it with a certain young lady in a nice place where nobody would think to look, so I'm afraid I'll have to ask you to find another dick to dirty your laundry, if you'll pardon my French."

Obermeier stared at him a moment, before removing the spectacles from the bridge of his nose, folding them up and placing them in the breast pocket of his suit.

"Mr. Ruby, you should know that our mutual friend, Miss Dixon, from the Boom-Boom Club is counting on your helping me with a little problem."

Rick felt the color drain from his face. He emptied his bourbon in a single gulp and smacked the glass down on the table hard enough to rattle Obermeier's battered old briefcase.

"What does Donna have to do with this business of yours?"

A faint smile played across Obermeier's face.

"The owner of the Boom-Boom Club happens to be an old family friend with a substantial investment in Monorail Pictures. These are tough times to be without a job, Mr. Ruby. Friends should do what they can to help one another remain gainfully employed, don't you think?"

"What I think, Junior, is that I'm beginning to dislike you and that you have my attention. Why don't we continue this conversation upstairs in my office where there are fewer distractions?"

Obermeier rose from his seat.

"Lead the way, Mr. Ruby.

Rick nodded and stood, paying one last glance at Evelyn's sensational legs on the stage in front of him before turning for the stairs. There wasn't much he could imagine better than Evelyn just about now.

Obermeier snapped the briefcase open revealing two long rows of freshly banded greenbacks.

Rick whistled appreciatively.

"Maybe my luck hasn't changed after all."

Obermeier smiled humorlessly again.

"One briefcase now, and another just like it when you finish the case."

Rick's mouth hung open as he stared at the money. He reached out and grabbed one of those stacks of green beauties and dragged his thumb across its edges delighting in its intoxicating aroma. These babies were far too rare these days to pass up, but it raised all sorts of questions.

"Exactly what is the case you want me to take for you, Mr. Obermeier?"

The thin man reached across and pulled the wad of bills from Ruby's hand and tossed it back into the briefcase.

"Are you familiar with Tulsa Blackie?"

Rick's brow furrowed.

"The cowboy star? I've heard of him. Who hasn't? What did he do, rob a bank?"

Obermeier paused for a beat.

"No, last night he took a dive into his penthouse swimming pool."

"Is there a law against it?"

"The pool was empty, Mr. Ruby. The coroner believes there was enough cocaine in Blackie's bloodstream to drug a bull elephant. Blackie was no coke fiend, Mr. Ruby. I know that for a fact. Someone decided to get rid of him. Someone has just cost Monorail Pictures an awful lot of money. This business is in my blood, Mr. Ruby. I negotiate with blackmailers, bootleggers, leg-breakers, and hookers every day of my life. This was something different. No warnings. No letters. No phone calls. Someone decided to remove our biggest star and I want their name. You play detective and finger the man for me, Mr. Ruby. We'll handle the rest."

"Why me? I'm a New Yorker. Why not get a dick with a suntan?"

"We need a dick without a leash, Mr. Ruby. A quickie, if you will. You say you're on vacation. I'm offering you a week in Hollywood, all expenses paid and you have my word that you'll be compensated generously."

"You flew all the way from Hollywood just for this?"

"I chartered a plane for the occasion this morning, Mr. Ruby. This is serious business, deadly serious. Tomorrow morning the story will be splashed all over the headlines. I want you in Hollywood where no one knows you, no one owns you, and no one suspects you of being on our payroll."

"And I have to finger the guy responsible within a week?"

Obermeier smiled.

"I certainly hope so, Mr. Ruby, for your sake. You see…my father is not a very patient man and he has a bad habit of throwing away tools that don't work right the first time. Now, if you're a very smart man, Mr. Ruby, you'll take this briefcase as a deposit. You'll put it someplace safe. You'll pack your things. Get a good night's sleep and meet me at the airfield at 5:00 AM sharp. Don't keep me waiting, Mr. Ruby. If there is one thing I value, it is punctuality."

"**W**hat kept you?"

The thin man with the glasses stood against the fence. Ruby had made the common mistake of misjudging Carl Obermeier based on his stature. He was his father's son through and through as he stood surveying Ruby like he was a piece of meat to be inspected.

"I had to post a letter and tie up some loose ends."

Rick pointed in the direction of the departing taxi.

"That would involve our faithful Miss Adams, I suppose."

Obermeier smiled faintly as Rick's face flushed.

"Don't look so surprised, Mr. Ruby. You knew I hadn't picked your name by random out of the Yellow Pages. I do my homework. I know all about your Girl Friday at the office as well as Miss Dixon and the lovely Miss St. Clair and even that bit of black tail from Belle's. It's a wonder it hasn't fallen off from overuse. You would feel right at home in Hollywood, Mr.

Ruby. Sex is the main form of currency. Topic A as one of my gauche poker friends calls it. Unfortunately for you, this is going to be a working holiday. I won't need you to take your pants off, just to keep your eyes open and your head clear. I trust you can manage that. Here, give me your other bag and let's not keep the pilot waiting any longer."

He reached for the smaller of Ruby's bags and the two men started toward the airfield where a private plane, paid by courtesy of Monorail Pictures, lie in wait for them.

Rick looked down upon the tiny squares of houses far below. From this distance they looked like Monopoly pieces, he thought. He was grateful for the distraction afforded by a gin and tonic and a fine Havana. If this was how Monorail treated their part-time help, maybe there was something in what Obermeier said about him feeling at home out in Hollywood. The climate would certainly be an improvement.

"Tell me some more about Blackie," Rick said, turning his attention away from the window as the plane began to climb up into the clouds.

Obermeier sat back in his seat and adjusted the tip of his fedora as he took a deep sigh.

"Nothing much to tell that hasn't already been splashed around in the trades or in the gossip columns…"

"You do realize regular folks like my Aunt Minnie don't read either, don't you?"

Obermeier smiled and bared a neat row of sharp little teeth in response to Rick's interruption.

"Nor do regular folks like your Aunt Minnie conceal guns in their shoulder straps when flying to the West Coast."

"You have a point," Rick chuckled. "Please continue with what you were saying."

"Blackie comes from a Hollywood family…"

"There seems to be a lot of that going around," Rick interjected.

"Do you mind if I lead?"

Rick smiled at this first sign that Carl Obermeier, Jr., might be a human being underneath it all.

Obermeier returned the smile and then continued.

"His mother made some pictures, but never made it to featured roles. The talkies killed her career. Great little body when she was in her prime, but the voice sounded like she needed an oil can."

"Are we talking squeaky as in Thelma Todd or pain-inducing as in Billie Burke?"

"I thought regular folks like your Aunt Minnie didn't read the trades."

"Very true, but they do go to the picture show and like to put names with faces…and legs."

"Sure, but this one had long since gone stale by the time picture shows were wired for sound."

"I figured as much, since Blackie's not exactly an ingénue. Wasn't he a stunt double for Astaire?"

"A double, but no stunts. He's your man if you need a nice shot of the back of his head…at least he was. The trouble started when he began believing he was an actor."

Rick shrugged." Who made him a leading man?"

"I did," Obermeier answered, "but that doesn't make him an actor. Just another schlep that looks good on a horse, that's all. Let us understand one another, Mr. Ruby. I know my father's studio turns out junk. If people want art, they'll turn to MGM. If they want entertainment, they'll look to Warners. The audience for Monorail's programmers are the kiddies who enjoyed the cartoon and the short and will be all tuckered out by the time the newsreel finishes and quite likely fast asleep or suffering the first twinge of a bellyache from eating too many Tootsie Rolls by the time our main feature plays."

"Okay, okay…you made your point, so he's no William Powell or Ronald Coleman, so what gives? Where do I start looking under rocks for who bumped off our talentless star?"

Obermeier stubbed out his cigar and carefully placed it inside the breast pocket of his seersucker suit.

"That's just the trouble. I don't have any leads to give you. If I did, I wouldn't need you. I'd take care of the problem myself."

"Like Daddy asked you to?"

Obermeier turned on Rick as if he'd been slapped.

"Where did you get that bright idea?"

"It was in all the gossip columns this morning."

Obermeier started to respond when the penny dropped and he caught a glimpse of Ruby's sly smile.

"A word of caution, Mr. Ruby. Monorail Pictures is giving you a car, a hotel, meals, expenses, and two nice new suitcases carefully packed with fresh new bills. Don't kill the golden goose by making a nuisance of yourself to my father. That means no advertising who hired you to stick your nose in Blackie's business."

"Won't that be obvious? You were his employer after all."

Obermeier paused before responding.

"Be creative, Mr. Ruby. Tell them you're investigating on behalf of Blackie's production company, Champlain-Blackie. They have a majority stake in the Tulsa Blackie pictures. Oh, there is one exception to this cover, of course."

"What is that?"

"When you sit down in J. C. Champlain's bungalow, you'll have to come up with a better line."

"No problem, I'll say I'm working for the family. Is the old broad still kickin'?"

"She is indeed. See, I knew you were the right man for the job, Mr. Ruby. Here."

He passed him a large manila envelope.

"Some reading material for you for the rest of the flight. Everything you could ever want to know about Tulsa Blackie. Names, addresses, and phone numbers. It's all there in black and white. Just like in the movies."

The first thing that struck Rick Ruby about Hollywood was the color. Gorgeous greens and blues. Deep blacks and silvers. Everything was new and well-polished. It was a chrome and leather paradise slick with surface gloss, but with no substance beneath it. A candy store where the candy came in just the right shape and sizes with your choice of blonde or brunette.

"Man, this is what I call livin'," Rick said as he picked up a newspaper at the front desk of his hotel.

TULSA BLACKIE'S LAST DIVE screamed the headline above a blurred snapshot of the bloodstained empty swimming pool in Blackie's penthouse. At least those bastards didn't get a photo of the body, Rick thought as he scanned the article for any interesting content. This being a newspaper, he wasn't surprised when the article amounted to four columns of nothing more than a bloated, error-filled summary of Blackie's short career and absolutely zip to add outside of stating he was dead and where and how he died.

"I'll never understand how people can read this rubbish with their morning coffee and still find the strength to go to work," Rick mumbled without looking up from the paper.

"Please tender a five-cent piece for that rubbish," the old grump behind the front desk rumbled, "this ain't a public library."

"No. No, it ain't," Rick said as he tossed him his nickel, "but it isn't much of a hotel, either. When Ricardo's done setting his hair, have him bring my bags and show me to my room, won't you, Cheerful?"

Neither the clerk nor the bellboy were much amused by his East Coast disposition, Rick noted. Geez, he understood Monorail Pictures not setting him up in the best of style, but he didn't expect no style at all. Junior must really be trying his best to stay under Daddy's line of vision.

The bellboy unlocked the door to his room and Rick was immediately assaulted by unpleasant reminders of other people's good times. Smoke, gin, and body sweat stained the walls, hung in the air, and clung to the sheets of the poorly made bed. The springs clanged loudly when Rick threw himself down on the mattress and stared at the slowly rotating blades of the ceiling fan as he felt his eyes grow heavy.

Rick was wide awake when the afternoon sun beat down upon the back of his neck as he stepped out onto the street. A few paces later and he climbed into the cherry red Packard and listened to the lovely sound of the engine turn over. A car was a luxury he could rarely afford and he was going to enjoy the sights and sounds of Los Angeles just as soon as he paid a visit to J. C. Champlain, screenwriter and Blackie's business partner.

The bungalow wasn't much but it was nicer than his hotel room, Rick thought as he entered the office fanning himself with his hat. Hair the color of burning flames were plastered across his damp forehead, drenched in perspiration. He knew he didn't look his best, but he didn't really see why that would matter when his aim was to speak with the gent who wrote Tulsa Blackie's adventures.

Then he saw the receptionist sitting behind her desk and instantly had cause to regret his disheveled appearance. Brown hair pulled back into a pony tail, big brown eyes, and a cute little nose. The pencil that rested between her teeth somehow made her look even more coquettish.

"May I help you?" she said, looking up at Rick's smiling face.

"I'm sure you can," he smirked, "I'm looking for Mr. Champlain."

"Mister?" she repeated the word as if puzzled.

"Ruby, Richard Ruby. You can call me Rick."

The knowing grin gave him some encouragement.

"Well, Rick, I'm afraid Mr. Champlain won't be able to see you."

He saw an opportunity here. Some definite possibilities if he played this cool.

"Well…will the old boy be in later? I certainly don't mind hanging around and, uh, admiring the view."

She smiled knowingly again and rested her chin in her hands, elbows perched before her on the desk. She was adorable.

"I'm afraid Mr. Champlain is late."

"Oh well, that's too bad, but, uh, hopefully we can find a way to while away the hours."

"Oh, I don't think Mr. Champlain would approve of that."

Oh, for crying out loud! He had to have a librarian for a receptionist.

"Well, if you ask me, I would be willing to bet that Mr. Champlain would want you to entertain an important client while he's away from the office."

He was leaning on the desk now, bent right over her. He could smell the perfume in her hair. Lilacs…she smelled like lilacs.

"Oh, but this isn't Mr. Champlain's office."

What? Who let this one out of Bellevue?

"Listen, doll, cut out the games. You said that Mr. Champlain couldn't see me because he was late."

"That's right, Rick."

Somehow he didn't like her being familiar with him now. It felt too much like there was a joke he wasn't in on yet.

"Then this is his office unless your command of the English language is somewhat different from the rest of us natives."

"How many of you are there?"

The eyes were wide and innocent as if it were a serious question.

"Cut it out, sister. No more foolin'. What gives?"

She threw back her head and laughed, clapping her hands delightedly. Rick felt his ears turning red. He was embarrassed and didn't know why, but he didn't like it one bit.

"I'm sorry, but it was too good to pass up. You need better material. Do receptionists really fall for corny approaches like that outside of books and movies?"

"Sometimes, yeah, they do! What of it?"

He was holding his hat now and ready to beat it. He was sick of being treated like a dumb kid. Goddamn Hollywood types always thinking they're so superior to real folks.

"I'm J. C. Champlain, the screenwriter. I'm afraid I have no use for a receptionist ,and Monorail doesn't pay well enough for me to afford one even if I had use for her. Mr. Champlain would be my father and he is late...as in deceased. You'll have to forgive me, but everyone always assumes a pretty young girl must be a secretary or somebody's girlfriend and certainly not a writer. Not that the screenplays I write count for much, but one day I'll get there. Do you know...I'm just about the only girl in this racket? Writing westerns, I mean."

"The Tulsa Blackie pictures?" Rick was calming down now.

"That's right. So tell me, Rick, why are you an important client if I've never heard of you?"

He was caught off guard for a moment and very nearly said he worked for Monorail just like her.

"The old lady hired me. Blackie's mom, that is."

"Mrs. Finster?"

She seemed troubled. Why was she troubled?

"That's strange. She didn't mention anything about hiring an investigator."

She seemed to put the thought out of her head for a moment and gave him her undivided attention.

"What is it you wish to ask me about Blackie, Mr. Ruby?"

Oh, so it was Mr. Ruby now. What was she hiding?

"Why should the old bird give you the good word about me? Isn't it enough to know that she sent me here?"

He was playing it well, but he had the distinct impression that good ol' Junior hadn't given him enough information in that manila envelope to carry this off convincingly.

"Well, she was like a mother-in-law to me," she drawled.

Mother-in-law? He definitely needed more information.

"Mother-in-law, huh? You don't seem much like the grieving widow at the moment."

She opened her mouth to reply, before her eyebrows arched and her mouth seemed to shrink to a perfect oval as her brow furrowed.

"Say...what kind of dick are you, anyway? There's no way that Mrs. Finster sent you over here without telling you about me and Blackie first."

"Did I say it was Mrs. Finster who hired me? You said it, sweetheart; I just went along for the ride."

"I'm not telling you nothin' before I talk to my mouthpiece. If you don't have a warrant, amscray."

She didn't actually say "amscray," but Rick didn't want to think about her using that kind of language unless it was in the form of a personal request.

❋ ❋ ❋

"**S**o I amscrayed," Rick finished, "that's all there was to it."

"Distinctly unimpressive, Mr. Ruby," was all that Obermeier said in response.

They were sitting in the bar at Rick's hotel. It was about ten at night and there was no one else around except for the bartender down at the other end of the bar listening to some goofy radio show.

"Well it's a little hard to impress when your file on the deceased fails to mention that America's Sweetheart was practically his wife."

Obermeier snorted, "No one ever accused J. C. Champlain of being America's Sweetheart, trust me. We had to feed that line about Blackie sharing an apartment with Mickey Rooney for fear that someone might find out about him and J. C."

"I don't follow you."

Obermeier drained his glass.

"J. C. is a girl."

"Yeah, I noticed the tight sweater. What's your point?"

"Blackie and J. C. were shacking up together," Obermeier's voice lowered to a conspiratorial whisper, "not the sort of thing your Aunt Minnie would approve of. Just the sort of thing that convinces parents to keep the kiddies away from the Tulsa Blackie pictures."

"Aunt Minnie can't have children."

"Never mind Aunt Minnie," Obermeier waved his hand dismissively, "Monorail doesn't need a scandal to make the goyim rail against Hollywood for corrupting the youth of America. They've done it before, they'll do it again, but they won't do it to this studio if you do your job right."

"So all that coke in Tulsa's bloodstream is not the sort of publicity you need."

"That's just the sort of publicity we're definitely not going to get," Obermeier poked him with a finger, "I've already taken steps to insure against that event. It wouldn't be much better to say he was drunk when he decided to try swimming sans water, unless you thought Prohibition did this country a bit of good."

"I'll drink to that."

"You'll do better than drink to it, you'll find his killer," again with the poking finger. "Someone's going to pay for Blackie's murder and you'll find him."

"What if it's a woman?"

"I don't care if it's a cocker spaniel. You get the goods and make it stick and you'll walk away with a nice retirement and I get to keep the family business intact. Do we understand each other?"

"Do we understand each other?" It was Rick's turn to get hot under the collar. "No, we don't understand each other. You let me walk into that barracuda's bungalow without telling me she was practically married to Tulsa. You okay some cockamamie story about Blackie's poor old mother hiring me to investigate her son's death without telling me that the old lady and the anaconda are as thick as thieves. That's not my idea of an understanding at all."

Obermeier looked like he was about to give an angry retort when he turned aside and wiped his wet lips dry. He stared into the empty glass and then pushed it away from him across the counter in the direction of the bartender and his radio.

"You're right, I was sloppy. I've never had to do this sort of thing before and I can't afford to let my father know all the facts yet. Once you find out who did it, then I can tell him what happened and how I handled it. But if I tell him now, he'll tear me to pieces."

"Well, that won't help either of us, will it? Give me the juice. Tell me everything there is to know about Tulsa Blackie. Where he was born, who his first girlfriend was, how he ever landed a gig playing himself instead of a character."

Obermeier smiled, "That was my idea. You remember Tom Mix, of course? Tom always played himself, never a character. When I first met Blackie I knew I could pull it off."

"Pull what off?"

Obermeier glanced down at his shoes for a second.

"Take an actor's double and turn him into a star for Monorail. We pay him peanuts, but it was a fortune next to working for scale as a double. The cute little girlfriend wanted to be a writer. Using her initials was her idea. Make everybody think that she pees standing up so as not to hamper her job opportunities. Clever kid, and just enough talent to write western hokum for us. The old man let them set up their own production company on the lot so as to reduce overhead. It gives them the illusion of independence and saves us a dime or two…or three or four. It worked well for awhile."

"Tell me everything you know about Tulsa Blackie."

"What went wrong?"

"What else?" Obermeier shrugged. "Even smart independent dames want to get married and raise a family sooner or later. Blackie knew a good thing when he saw it and he didn't want to see it end, so he stopped coming home at night. We tried to help things out, stop her from feeling so lonely, but she wouldn't have any of it. Stars, directors, producers, executives, even me. Not anybody. Just her Blackie. The bust-up wasn't pretty, but we had them both under contract so their professional partnership outlasted the sex."

"That's a nice little melodrama, but I saw her this afternoon. The mascara hasn't been running."

"She's not the grieving type. She's made of cast iron. Fiercely loyal, too. She got sore at you probably because she's protective of the old lady."

"Mrs. Finster?"

Obermeier nodded, "That's right."

"I'm still not buying. Her dander was up because she didn't want me asking questions of her. I know self-interest when I see it, and when it comes to dames, you can bet they always know at least two things: just how pretty they are and what's in it for them."

Obermeier motioned the bartender for a refill. The man tore himself away from the radio with an effort.

"So what now, Sherlock?"

"Now I sleep on it and figure out if I take candy and flowers to the shrew or dig up Grandma and see if six feet of muscle and easy love will loosen her parched lips any."

"And people think I do unconscionable things for a paycheck."

"It's the American Dream, Junior. The Almighty Dollar has no tolerance for scruples."

"I'll drink to that, Brother Ruby."

Obermeier chuckled as he downed his drink in one gulp.

"Come on, I'd better walk you to your car while you can still see straight."

Obermeier hesitated for a moment and glanced at his watch.

"Maybe you're right. It's later than I thought."

"It always is when there's a corpse involved…or a pretty wife at home."

Obermeier looked at him sharply, but Rick only smiled.

They stepped out onto the pavement and Rick welcomed the cool night air as the only antidote to the steaming humidity that never seemed to escape the hotel either day or night.

He was just about to say something to Obermeier when a squeal of car tires made him turn. Out of the corner of his eye, he saw the muzzle of a Tommy gun aiming right at them. Without thinking, he knocked Obermeier to the ground and threw himself on top of him.

Bullets tattooed on the brick wall just inches above Rick's back. He kept his head low until the ringing in his ears subsided and he found the courage to peek his head up. There was no sign of the car, but a small crowd was nervously gathering across the street.

"Let's go," he snapped at Obermeier as he helped him to his feet.

"What the hell was that about?"

Rick shrugged, "Maybe your wife is sick of you staying out all night with rugged, good-looking men like me."

Obermeier shook his head, "More likely somebody knows what we're up to and wants to make sure Blackie's file stays closed."

They reached Obermeier's car. Rick looked around nervously while the thin man climbed in behind the wheel.

"You bring up a good point, Junior, what about the cops? Aren't they looking into Blackie's death, too?"

"Whaddya think I was born yesterday, maybe? The cops were the first ones I paid off. It's not even corrupt in this town. They come and ask you first. I have tremendous respect for the Irish."

"Yeah, yeah, they're the Lost Tribe. Isn't there anybody in this town that can't be bought?"

Obermeier smiled, "That's a mighty strange question for a private dick to ask, Mr. Ruby."

"Maybe you're right about that, Junior," Rick said quietly, "maybe you're right."

Rick was exhausted when he climbed the stairs to the third floor. He felt a slight pang of relief when he saw "325" on the door to his apartment. It was home for now. He unlocked the door and stepped inside.

Shutting and locking the door behind him, he took eight steps forward until the bed was visible in the darkness through the glint of the streetlight that shone through the blinds. He reached a hand up and pulled the chain, illuminating the room with the single light bulb that hung from the ceiling fixture.

His eyes adjusted to the absence of darkness after a second. He glanced around the room and sniffed the air again as he had when he first entered. Damn, he was tired. He yawned as he took off his jacket and shoulder strap and laid them both gingerly upon the bed. He stretched and yanked the undershirt off. Covered in perspiration, the shirt bunched as he pulled it over his head. He let it drop on the ground as he undid the clasp of his belt and pulled it off his waist while he walked toward the little bathroom.

He was whistling "Easy to Love" as he pulled the slack end of the belt through the clasp, careful not to let the pin hook through any of the holes. He bent over the tub and turned on the hot water and then pulled the curtain all the way over and backed up slowly against the wall right behind the door.

He didn't have long to wait before the bathroom door creaked open. The first thing he saw was the barrel of a gun and then the gloved hand holding it. He set his jaw firmly and tried not to listen to his heart pounding in his ears as a man, dressed in a rumpled grey suit stepped cautiously into the bathroom and approached the tub.

Steam from the hot water poured out around the curtain. Rick held his breath. This had better work because he'd only get one chance. Silent as a panther stalking a rival predator, he stepped from behind the bathroom door and slung his belt like a lasso around the neck of the armed man while simultaneously lifting his leg and placing his foot at the small of the man's back and kicking forward.

The man stumbled head-first into the curtain as Rick pulled back on the belt which tightened around the man's throat. He heard him gasp in shock. Rick swung his left leg forward and knocked the man off his feet. They both fell forward tearing the curtain down off its rod. Using his free arm, Rick held the man's left wrist, pointing the gun at the wall.

"Drop it or I break your wrist."

Rick counted two seconds. No response. He slammed the wrist hard against the bathtub. There was a crunching of bone before the gun clattered to the floor. Rick bent his knee forward to enable his left shoe to reach the gun and push it across the bathroom tiles out of harm's way. Grabbing the belt with his right hand, he tightened the hold on the man's throat.

He listened to the sound of choking and coughing, then released the belt and tipped the man forward into the tub, keeping his head underwater for ten seconds. He pulled him out. The man fought for breath. Rick tightened the hold on the belt until he started choking again. He released the hold and dunked him underwater for another ten seconds. He pulled him back up and started to tighten the belt.

"No more, please!" the man wheezed, water dripping from his nose as if it were a leaky faucet.

"Give me one good reason why I shouldn't drown you or strangle you?" Rick snarled.

"I wasn't going to kill you!" the man was still gasping, trying to catch his breath.

"Yeah, I said to myself, I bet that gun isn't anything more than a scare tactic," Rick sneered.

He tightened his hold on the belt again. The man's face was now turning purple. Rick released his hold after only five seconds.

"Start talking or you go under again."

"I work for Lillian Finster. She told me to come and fetch you."

"Yeah, did she tell somebody else to bump me off first? I was nearly gunned down outside in the parking lot a few minutes ago, so I'm afraid that you bore the brunt of it."

"I don't know nothin' 'bout any of that...I swear it! I was just told to bring you back to Mrs. Finster is all."

Rick paused to think things over. "Lucky for you that you have an honest face." Letting go of the belt, he grabbed the man by the collar and a pant leg and hauled him face first into the tub with a splash. Rick scrambled for the discarded gun so that by the time the half-drowned rat found his feet and clambered out of the tub, he had him covered.

"Where's the Finster broad live?"

"47 Wachovia Lane in Pasadena."

"Where are your car keys?"

"In..in my pants pocket," he answered nervously.

"Take 'em off. Take everything off. Every last stitch of clothing."

"What? Here?"

"That's right, Bashful, here and be quick about it unless you want a couple extra orifices."

Rick waited until the man stripped and then he motioned him out of the bathroom. Once outside, he made him get down on his knees and cover his head while Rick retrieved his holster and jacket from the bed. He didn't have time to grab a new undershirt from the suitcase jammed under the bed.

"Get up!" Rick yelled to him.

Shaking like a leaf, the naked man rose to his feet.

"Unlock the door."

The man paused, "You're...you're making me go out in the hall like this?"

"That's right, Cutie-pie. It's time for you to make new friends by showing off your birthday suit. Get out in that hall and go down the steps you snuck up before. And if you even think about turning around before you're on the street, so help me God, I'll drill you where you stand, understand me?"

"But...but I'll get arrested if I go out like this!"

"Would you like one asshole or two? It's your choice, Sweetie."

The dumb cluck gulped and made his choice.

It was after midnight by the time Rick made it out to Pasadena. He found the place alright. Forty-seven Wachovia Lane. The same address Obermeier had in his file. The street was dark, but there was still a light on in the back of the house. He let himself in the front door using the keys he took from the goon's pants pockets.

No dogs. So far so good, he thought to himself.

He heard the sound of voices from the back of the house where the light was lit. He made his way forward cautiously with the goon's gun in his hand. As he neared the kitchen, the first thing he realized was that the voices he had heard were coming from a radio, the second was the crack of light shining underneath the door.

"Is that you, Freddie?"

The voice belonged to an old woman who had spent too many hours each day with cigarettes and whiskey for company.

Rick came through the kitchen door with the gun pointing in front of him.

"Freddie got picked up by the cops for running around without any clothes on so I told him I'd keep my date with you anyway. I'm Rick Ruby. I'm the private dick trying to find out who bumped off your son."

Rick wasn't sure what to expect in response, but he didn't expect the old lady to look at him with genuine surprise and then evident amusement as she let out a wheezing laugh that sounded like it might be contagious and possibly terminal. She reached a bony hand forward and switched off the radio.

"I'm Lillian Finster, Mr. Ruby. Please have a seat. I assure you I'm unarmed."

Just to prove her point she opened her bathrobe for him. What he saw was old and well-worn but probably still recently serviced. He may have just done old Freddie a favor by getting him locked up for the night.

"What say we talk about your boy, Blackie?" Rick asked as he sat down at the kitchen table across from her.

"Can I get you a drink, Mr. Ruby? Coffee? Whiskey?"

"Let's stick with answers. How about how did you find out about me and more importantly, how did you track me down so quickly?"

"Joanna told me all about you. She called me as soon as you left her," the voice quivered as she spoke, but the eyes were steady and the mind behind them was still sharp. The smile that flickered around the corners of her mouth was anything but good-natured.

"Joanna? Who? Oh, you mean J. C."

She nodded her head slowly, "You catch on quick, Pretty Boy."

"Say, uh…what exactly is the deal…was the deal with her and your son?"

"She loved him." the statement was simple and direct, but she couldn't help but titter once it slipped out of her mouth. "The little fool really loved him…once. Not now, of course. No woman can love once she's been cut to the quick, but she did love him for a time."

She shook her head bemusedly. "That's more than I could ever give him."

"Well, you were only his mother…"

The eyes blazed like burning coals. This one wasn't so besotted that she didn't understand when she was being insulted or judged.

"Yes, I was only his mother, or rather, he was only my child. I had a career, Mr. Ruby, a dream. I had it within reach. The key. The ring. The prize. It was mine for the taking…until my husband had to come along and screw it all up."

"How's that?"

She shook her head irritably, "Not my Harold, the late Mr. Finster…." she pronounced the latter with mock reverence; "I'm talking about my first husband. Jackie's real father."

"Jackie?"

"Yes, Jackie. Blackie was what I called him as a boy. Blackie Jackie. My little black sheep. My poor little unwanted lamb."

She broke down into tears. Rick leaned forward and touched her hand. She pulled her arm back as if his touch was deadly.

"Don't you dare pity me," she thundered through clenched teeth. She sat there, breathing heavily, just staring at him until she regained control of herself again.

"How did Jackie's father screw everything up?"

Her eyes refocused as her memories traveled back down avenues she had left far behind with no intention of ever seeing again.

"When I left Jack, I left the boy with him. I didn't belong with them." She shook her head and made a sour face. "Not in that house, not with that woman – his mother." She pronounced the word as if it were obscene. "I wasn't an Okie like the rest of 'em," she laughed, and the sound was sharp and cold.

"An Okie? Oh, I see…Tulsa Blackie."

She seemed to notice him again at last. She nodded and gave him a crooked grin.

"See? I said you catch on quick."

"So Jack…raised Jackie…until he came out to Hollywood and found you."

The eyes wandered again as she relived ugly scenes from her past.

"That's right. He found me. 'Take the boy, Lillian; I can't raise him by myself. Take him; give him the same chance as you.' What chance?"

She pulled a cigarette from the pack on the table in front of her and lit it, taking a deep breath and letting the smoke snake from her mouth and nostrils in trailing wisps that vanished as they climbed for the stars.

"And Harold…" she cackled again, "Harold, bless him, he adopted him. He thought if he paid Jack to go away all would be well. Give Jackie his name and make him part of the family. Make us a family is what he wanted. Sentimental fool. He didn't know the half of it. I knew. I had left once before, but I couldn't leave again. There was no where left to go. I just waited for Harold to die and now…Jackie's gone, too and there's just me."

"Who killed your son, Mrs. Finster?"

She stubbed the cigarette out.

"This town killed my son, Mr. Ruby. Can you arrest a whole town? They're guilty. Every one of them…those sons of bitches. They're all guilty. His blood, Harold's blood, your blood, my blood, it's on all of their hands. How do you stop it, Mr. Ruby? It's an infection. Everybody wants it, but it kills and everyone believes they'll be the lucky ones who survive. They'll be different from all the rest."

"You know I had the exact same conversation with the Ladies Guild once about temperance."

She laughed and looked him up and down.

"You'd like Tulsa, Mr. Ruby. Yes indeed, you'd fit right in with all those other fine upstanding people."

"So J. C. called you about me. How did you tail me so fast?"

"I didn't. J. C. did. She followed you herself and called me from a phone booth across the street from your hotel. She's a smart girl ,or you're a stupid jackass of a detective for not picking up a tail like that."

"Somebody tried to kill me in the parking lot just a few minutes before Freddie came waltzing into my room with a gun to invite me to this dance."

"I sent Freddie to retrieve you, certainly, but if I wanted you dead, you would be dead, Mr. Ruby. And I can think of a lot more pleasant things to do to you than kill you." The old shark showed her teeth again. Ruby felt like a tuna who wandered away from his school.

"If you didn't put the mark on me, then who did? Who else knows about me except you and J. C.?"

"Well, there's whoever hired you, Mr. Ruby."

"Uh-uh. Wrong answer. I can't explain why, but it wasn't the party that hired me that told somebody to bump me off."

"You want to get to the bottom of this thing, Mr. Ruby? You really want to know what's what?"

Rick nodded his head slowly.

"Burn the whole goddamn town to the ground. Cleanse this paradise in the sun and start over again like God after the Great Deluge. Wash away the filth and the lies and the blood and the dirty little secrets and start clean."

"That's your answer, huh? Hollywood is the guilty party."

"That's my answer, Mr. Ruby," she said leaning forward. "Now what about yours?"

※ ※ ※

Rick was happy to get out of the house with his family jewels intact and untouched. Somebody had to tell that old broad she was about twenty years too late to play those games, but it wasn't going to be him, brother. Let some other sap tell that man-hungry old tiger it was time to retire. It wasn't going to be him. Not while she still had teeth.

It was late and he was wired from the events of the evening. Sleep was out of the question. He could just drive aimlessly since Monorail Pictures was paying for the gas, but he didn't think that would help relax him either. He knew what he wanted to do. He wanted to take a ride over to Blackie's penthouse apartment and scout around. The place must have a cordon thrown around it with cops and reporters snooping everywhere, but he could be just one more morbid curiosity seeker out to grab a thrill. Maybe that's all a private detective was anyway.

When he arrived at the address in the file, he found it wasn't what he was expecting. There may have been a penthouse apartment with an indoor swimming pool, but this was a far cry from the Fountain Bleu. Tulsa Blackie wasn't a star in any real sense except in the eyes of undiscriminating nine-year-olds. He was just a two-bit actor who had made good in a town that was filled to the brim with more of the same. There were no crowds, no police, and no press to be found. The body had long since been removed and the scene of his death had already been gone over with a fine tooth comb. Now there was nothing but an empty locked apartment. A cold reminder, like a tombstone at a grave no one bothers to visit.

Getting upstairs had not taken too much effort. The West Coast definitely seemed more lax than New York if a second rate joint like this was anything to judge, he thought. Rick wrapped his left hand in his handkerchief and reached a hand out to try the door to Blackie's apartment.

What was he doing wasting his time here? What did he expect to find?

"You lookin' for somethin', buddy?"

The voice sounded pleasant, but not in a good way. It was the sort of voice that says I'm looking for an excuse to do you severe harm and the second you turn your head and look at me is my invitation to turn you into raw meat.

"Yeah, I'm with the water company. Somebody called to get the water turned back on so they could fill up the swimming pool," Rick replied.

He didn't bother to glance behind him since he was pretty sure that the face that went with the voice was ugly and the hand that belonged to the body that went with the voice was the one sticking the gun in his back at the moment.

"Say, that's pretty funny," the voice didn't sound amused. "You shoulda thought about tellin' jokes for a living instead of snoopin' around where you don't belong. You might have lived longer, chump."

"I'm going to take a wild guess and say you are not an associate of Freddie's."

Rick kept his eyes in front of him.

"I missed once, pal, I don't intend to miss a second time," the voice grunted.

"That was my second guess."

Rick started to turn around. There was no avoiding the outcome this time, but he might as well go down fighting, he thought, or rather he was starting to think when the butt of the gun caught him square in the back of the skull. He had a vague sensation of the walls and doors in the corridor starting to swim, and then blackness swallowed him whole.

※ ※ ※

He awoke with the dawning awareness of a recurring dream where he was a loser stuck in a town where everyone else was an even bigger loser.

Aw crap, he struggled to think through his splitting headache and jumbled awareness of reality, it wasn't a dream. This was his life. God, he was tired of getting knocked out. One of these days someone was going to do him permanent harm if they hadn't already.

"Glad you're not dead."

The voice sounded matter of fact and decidedly female.

Rick fought to stop his vision from blurring. He shook his head. That hurt. Don't do that twice, he thought.

The room came into focus. It was small. No furnishing. One window. Blinds pulled closed. Little light coming through. It was early morning, he guessed. There was a dame in the corner by the window. She was looking at him. She was pretty badly bruised. One eye was swollen nearly shut. There was a cut on her cheek. Her skirt and her blouse had tears in them.

"You don't recognize me?"

He gingerly shook his head no.

"Joanna Champlain."

Still a blank.

"J. C. Champlain. You came to see me, remember?"

Oh, Christ, it was her, he thought.

"Where are we? What happened to you?"

She sighed and looked up at the ceiling.

"We're in a cabin in the woods about an hour's drive outside Hollywood. Connelly's goon brought us here."

"Who is Connelly?"

She shook her head.

"You really are a third-rate detective, aren't you? Whoever hired you really should have been less concerned with saving money and more concerned with getting their money's worth. Jack Connelly was Blackie's real father."

Rick attempted to climb to his feet, but stumbled.

"The old man killed his own son? Why?"

Joanna looked at him and laughed, shaking her head sadly.

"Why are most crimes committed? Greed. Champlain-Blackie has a 35-percent ownership stake in all of the Tulsa Blackie pictures. When things went south for me and Blackie, he made his father...his real father... his sole beneficiary."

"Were they close?"

She laughed at the question.

"He hadn't seen him in more than twenty years. He was just a kid when his dad brought him out to Hollywood and dumped him with his mother."

"What did the old man do after that?"

She shrugged.

"He went back to Tulsa and drank away the family fortune. Old Oklahoma oil money. The well ran dry. The money spent…he needed more. So he wrote to Blackie to hit him up for cash."

She laughed again.

"Blackie didn't have any cash to give him. It was all tied up in the pictures. 'We bankroll what we earn, baby, and when it comes home to roost, we'll be millionaires!' To think that I believed him at the time."

She shook her head at the memory.

"That's all water under the bridge now…maybe two bridges."

"I think I understand the rest. Blackie didn't have anyone in his life any more. Not you, not his Mom, not even the stepfather who adopted him. He couldn't disappoint the old man when he hit him up for cash so he told him he had made him his sole beneficiary and the old man decided to hurry things along."

She nodded her head ruefully.

"You may make the grade yet, pal. He slipped him a Mickey. Shot him up with cocaine and talked him into taking a swim to clear his head. I can just imagine the conversation, Blackie was always one to rave about reaching greater heights. I sat through that scene so many times I could have written it. That ham probably thought he was on a movie set when he made the big dive. He always wanted to be Johnny Weissmuller or Buster Crabbe. It was his big moment to dive for the Olympic Gold."

Rick just stared at her while she spoke.

"You must have really hated him."

Her eyes met his.

"After the endless humiliation. One affair after another. Animal, vegetable, or mineral…whatever he convinced himself would advance his career. Yes, I learned to hate him…but not as much as I hate Connelly for what he did to me."

Rick looked at the cuts and bruises and the torn clothes.

"He forced himself on you?"

She shrugged.

"You get used to it in this town. Fathers-in-law, producers, studio executives. What's mine is yours. A girl learns to wash up and keep quiet if she wants to keep working. It could be worse, I could have been an actress instead of just a lowly screenwriter."

Rick looked around the room.

"So why are we here?"

"We're stashed here until his goon comes back for us. Then he'll kill us. Got any ideas on how to change the ending, bright boy?"

He reached for his shoulder strap, but found it and the gun were gone.

"I'll think of something."

Rick didn't have long to think. Just a few minutes later, a squeal of tires and a slamming of two car doors were heard.

"He's back!" Joanna sounded genuinely terrified. "There was a second door! That means Connelly is with him! My God, this is it. We're going to die."

The sound of a door creaking open, two sets of footsteps leading to just outside the room. A key in the lock and then the door opened and two men entered. The first man was abnormally tall with large, misshapen features. The second was an older man, well-dressed but smelling strongly of liquor.

"Oh, good…the kids are still awake," the goon said with a smile.

He walked over to Joanna and stood above her, legs spread wide with his hands buried deep in his pockets.

"And how is my favorite playmate this morning?"

"That's quite enough, Gilbert," the old man chided, "you'll give us a reputation. Now I hope you've had time to reconsider my generous offer, my dear. For your sake and for the sake of your boyfriend here."

He nodded his head in Rick's direction.

"Perhaps if Gilbert breaks the nice man's fingers, you will be more co-operative, hmm?"

"The nice man's fingers don't mean a thing to her," the goon said with a sneer. "It's my fingers she likes."

Joanna spat at his face, but only reached his stomach. Gilbert looked down on her and laughed and then delivered a sharp kick to her right calf. She rolled to her side in pain.

"I want my son's rights, Miss Champlain. Now you either sign willingly or we'll do it the hard way. What's it going to be?"

Joanna told the old man something creative that amused Gilbert, but did little to help the old man's mood.

"Gilbert, break Miss Champlain's arm, please."

It's now or never, Rick told himself. He struggled to his feet, surprisingly quiet for a big man, and half-fell against the old man's back. An arm snaked around Connelly's neck. Rick used his free hand to grasp his left hand and secure it, like a vise, around the old man's throat.

"Call your dog off, Connelly or you're a dead man."

Gilbert spun round and took in the scene quickly. Connelly clawed at Rick's arms, but could not budge them. It was evident the old man was fighting to breathe and could not control his racing heart.

Gilbert laughed, "You think you hold all the cards, do you?"

Rick released his grip on the arm around the old man's neck and with his free hand grabbed the side of Connelly's face, digging his pinkie finger into Connelly's right eye. The old man screamed and began flailing about, but Ruby held firm and did not release the grip around his throat or let go of his head.

"Should I pop the eye out of its socket or do you back away from the girl?"

The old man had started hyperventilating. Rick loosened his grip and let him slip limply to the floor. Gilbert crossed the room to the old man's side, Rick backed away from them and edged nearer toward where the girl lay on the floor against the window.

Unsteadily, he bent down and reached out a hand to help her to her feet.

With a shaking hand, she pointed to the back seat of the goon's pants where the handle of his gun was protruding. Rick barely paused to consider what would happen if he failed. He moved forward, silent as a panther. He was grateful for the old man's labored breathing as it was the only cover he had as he reached behind Gilbert and quickly pulled the gun free from his back pocket.

The larger man spun and started to lift a hand toward Rick when the detective brought the muzzle of the gun down hard against Gilbert's left temple as his head turned toward him. The goon crumpled to the floor as the old man's wheezing grew unbearable and then abruptly ceased.

J. C. was at his side and reaching a shaking hand toward him.

"Give me the gun. You check on Connelly."

Rick hesitated for a second or two and then handed her the gun before crouching down and placing his ear against the old man's chest.

"He's dead." Rick started to say, but the second word was drowned out by the ear-splitting sound of two gunshots. Gilbert's head sprayed across the floor in a garish mix of red and black as his face crumpled like a deflating paper bag.

"What the hell did you do that for, you crazy broad?" Rick shouted as he

"Call your dog off, Connelly, or you're a dead man."

grabbed the still-smoking gun out of J. C.'s hands.

She stood there trembling as she stared down at Gilbert's corpse. Tears streaked her face. She seemed unsteady on her feet and her breath came in little gasps while her lower lip quivered.

"They both deserve to be dead," was all that she said, never lifting her eyes from Gilbert's ghastly corpse.

"So does Hitler. So does Mussolini. So do a lot of people, but nobody does it when they're sleeping, do they? There is such a thing as honor."

She turned on him, savagely and dug her nails into the torn blouse and ripped it open exposing the black brassiere beneath.

"You want to tell me about honor? When did they treat me with anything but contempt? When did anyone ever do differently by me. I'm sick of being someone else's sorry excuse for an existence. I'm sick of myself."

The sound of sirens cut through the early morning and grew steadily louder.

Rick crossed to the window and pulled the blinds sideways, shielding his eyes from the punishing rays of sun.

Two squad cars were racing up the drive toward the cabin.

"Looks like we have company," Rick groaned.

Rick tossed the gun over by the door and placed his hands on his head. He edged a safe distance away from the window.

Three minutes that felt like an eternity passed when four police officers, guns held at ready, burst through the door.

"Jesus Christ!" a kid that looked too young to be a cop swore. "What the hell happened here?"

"Looks like somebody lost their head," an older officer said glumly, lowering his weapon and carefully retrieving the gun from the floor.

"Murder weapon – bag it," he said turning to the officer at his side. "Turn around, sonny, hands against the wall and spread 'em."

Rick did as he was told. The frisk was quick and professional. He felt his wallet pulled from his back pocket.

"Well, well…a private dick," the older cop didn't sound like the friendly type. "Tell me something useful, Richard."

"Not my gun and I didn't pull the trigger. You'll find my prints on it all the same."

The cop laughed. "Interesting, but not what I would call exactly useful. Why don't you try useful before I try my hand at persuading you?"

"I shot him."

The cop spun and looked over at Joanna. Another officer was tending to her injuries and stood there frozen with shock at her unexpected statement.

"What about the old guy?"

She turned to look down at another officer crouching over Connelly's corpse.

"His heart gave out in all the excitement," Rick said.

"Even more interesting," the cop smirked. "Keep talking, Bright Eyes, and maybe you'll make it to useful yet."

"You remember that cowboy star found dead at the bottom of an empty swimming pool in his penthouse apartment a few days ago?"

"Which one?" A cop at the door asked sarcastically. His partner next to him nudged him in the ribs.

"The old-timer was his father."

"Congratulations, you made it to useful. Keep talking."

"I know more than he does."

Rick raised his eyebrows.

The cop turned to Joanna, "Do continue, sister. We haven't anything better to do this morning."

"Mind if I smoke?" she asked. The officer next to her reached into his shirt pocket and handed her a pack of Lucky Strikes. She shook a cigarette loose and handed the pack back to him. The cop fished a matchbook out of his pants pocket and struck the match for her. She steadied his big hand with her small one as he lit her cigarette. She blew smoke out of the corner of her mouth away from his direction and thanked him.

"The old man was Jack Connelly of Tulsa, Oklahoma. Like the man said, he was Tulsa Blackie's natural father. His parents broke up when Blackie was just a kid. His mom came out here for the usual reasons and got hitched to a guy named Harold Finster who ended up adopting Blackie when the old man dumped him with his Mom after the family's oil field dried up."

"Another Hollywood Happy Ending," the cop next to Rick murmured.

"It gets better," Joanna continued, "twenty-odd years pass. Blackie goes from an extra to a cowboy star. He hitched his wagon next to mine and I wrote the pictures for him."

"No foolin'?" The cop next to her asked.

"All by myself. Girls don't just type, you know; some of them can make up stories, too. Anyway, me and Blackie split up on account of his playing hide the sausage in every warm bun he could find, but we still had the baby to take care of…the baby being our production company that produces the great works of genius that are the Tulsa Blackie pictures.'

"So along comes Jack Connelly without a cent to his name looking for Blackie to make good with the old man who abandoned him. So what does the big lug do? Having just sunk his last dollar into the next picture we're supposed to make, he tells the old man he's named him his sole beneficiary. You see Blackie is big on fortune tellers...tea leaves...the whole nine yards. Some yokel that soaks him dry told him he would die before he turned forty and he believed the bunk."

"Sounds like maybe it wasn't the bunk," the cop next to her said.

"Shut up, Hannigan!" the cop next to Rick growled. "Go on, sister, we're still awake."

"So the old man decides to move things along. He's the one who shot Blackie full of cocaine that night he made his last dive. Blackie had many faults, but cocaine wasn't one of them."

"I never read anything about cocaine in the newspaper," the cop next to her opened his trap again.

"Shut it, Hannigan."

Joanna smiled and dropped her cigarette to the floor and stubbed it out with her shoe.

"That's not the end of it. Connelly turns up right after Blackie dies and tells me that it's in my best interest to turn over all controlling interests in Champlain-Blackie, that was our production company, to him. He seemed to think it would be bad for my health to keep running it on my own."

"So you did the smart thing and called a private dick instead of the cops, is that right?"

"Is that right, Rick?" Joanna asked with a faint smile on her lips.

"You're doing the talkin', kiddo. You don't need pointers from me."

The cop next to Rick rolled his eyes, "Swell, he thinks he's a flatfoot but at least he knows he isn't bright enough to be a mouthpiece."

"I know you think I should have gone to the proper authorities..." Joanna paused, choosing her words carefully, "...but sometimes there are extenuating circumstances."

"Ah, I think I see..." the older cop said. "The old man had some dirt on you that you couldn't afford to get out."

"And people say all cops are dumb," Rick smirked.

"Shut up, wiseguy. Go on with your story."

"We ended up here. The guy with no face was called Gilbert. I never knew his last name. He was Connelly's hired muscle. He picked up Ruby nosing around Blackie's apartment and brought him here with me. It was looking like curtains for both of us when Rick did what he was paid to do and got me out of a jam."

"And you shot Gilbert?" The older cop asked.

Joanna nodded, "It was him or me. What would you have done?"

The cop snorted loudly and turned to Rick, "Do you agree with her account of how things happened?"

"Me?" Rick asked, incredulously, "Since when does anyone trust the word of a private dick about anything?"

The old cop grimaced, "Now you're neither useful nor interesting. Bring 'em both down to the station to give their statements. Somebody get an ambulance out here for the two stiffs."

"I've got one question for you."

The old cop turned toward Rick with a look of genuine surprise on his face.

"Me? What can I tell you?"

"You could start by explaining how you found us here in the first place."

The cop smirked at him, "That's easy. Monorail Pictures reported a stolen automobile and said they believed the killers behind Tulsa Blackie's murder were behind the car theft. They gave us an address where they thought we might find the vehicle and the killers so we came prepared. Does that square with you?"

"Yeah," Rick mumbled, "it squares with me just swell."

"**T**hat was a swell job, gumshoe," Obermeier said as he handed over a second suitcase full of crisp new Benjamin Franklins. "See Irene on your way out and she'll make arrangements for your flight back to New York. Now if you don't mind, I have work to do so, no offense, but hopefully I won't be needing you again."

Obermeier sat down and started looking over a memo from his father. He looked up after a minute and saw Ruby sitting there, staring at him with a blank look on his face.

"I hope there isn't a problem, Mr. Ruby."

Rick stared at him another minute and then said, "I hope so, too."

He stood and walked out of the office. Obermeier breathed a sigh of relief and rubbed his forehead wearily.

Irene was as good as Obermeier's word and had set Rick up nicely. He had one more night at the crummy hotel and then he would leave the Packard at the air field in the morning and be on his way back to New York. He finished his coffee, checked out of the hotel and climbed in behind the wheel of the car.

"Hello, Dreamboat."

Rick's heart skipped a beat as he glanced in the rear view mirror and saw a familiar face in his backseat with a gun level with the back of his head. The wrist holding the gun was heavily bandaged.

"Freddie!"

"Aw, how sweet! You remembered me!"

Freddie reached forward with his good hand and grabbed a handful of Rick's red hair and twisted his head down sideways.

"Do you know what I am going to do to you, Sweetie?"

Rick swallowed hard, "Make me strip and walk down the street naked until I get picked up by a cop?"

Freddie shook his head, "Nah, something more original. I'm going to cut off both your hands and let you bleed to death from your wrists. And you know the best part?"

Rick stared at the glove compartment, feeling incredibly stupid.

"There's a better part?"

Freddie laughed. "Sure there is, Cutie-pie. The best part is once you've bled to death, I'm going to pour gasoline on you and set you on fire."

"You know what I think, Freddie?"

"Tell me what you think, Ruby?"

"I think you don't like me very much, and that strikes me as very surprising indeed."

Freddie laughed again, "Why should that surprise you, you stupid dick?"

Rick just about managed to shrug his shoulders from his awkward position. "Probably because you seem like the sort of guy who usually likes dicks."

"Why, you little…"

Freddie let go of Rick's hair and shoved his head down deep into the passenger seat with his good hand across Rick's left cheek. The big man leaned over the front seat and shoved his pistol under Rick's nose.

Ruby stretched forward and bit into Freddie's pistol hand.

The big man let go of the pistol with a gasp of pain. The gun clattered against Rick's face and fell to the floor in front of the passenger seat.

Ruby twisted his head sideways and bit down savagely at Freddie's good hand. Rick was bleeding profusely from where the pistol had struck the bridge of his nose. The blood from his nose mixed with the blood from the half-severed finger on Freddie's right hand until Rick feared he was going to choke on all of the blood pouring into his mouth.

Freddie howled in pain and grasped his newly-injured hand.

Rick placed both his hands against the passenger door and lifted his body up with his left leg and swung viciously with his right leg delivering a sharp kick into the right side of Freddie's jaw.

He heard the crunch of teeth and smiled as he hurled himself over the front seat and knocked Freddie sideways down on the back seat with Ruby landing astride the big man. He began wailing on Freddie's face again and again until the flesh became soft and he felt his knuckles tear against the jagged roughness of a shattered cheekbone.

Exhausted and panting, he caught his breath long enough to realize that Freddie was unconscious and probably near death. His heart was pounding in his chest. He felt half-drunk from the rush of adrenalin. He climbed off of Freddie and climbed back into the front seat of the cherry red Packard and turned the key in the ignition.

He was still panting when he pulled into the lot at Monorail Pictures. He hoped the guard at the gate wouldn't glance in the backseat.

✳ ✳ ✳

It was nearly ten in the morning before Obermeier arrived at the office. He said good morning to Irene and told her to fix him a coffee and bring him the morning paper in fifteen minutes. He opened the door and stepped in his office.

The first thing he noticed were the lights. Why were the lights on? He'd have to fire that stupid Mexican woman, how many times did he have to tell her? Wait a minute! Why the hell were there two cans of gasoline on his desk?

Two cans of...

His head spun to the chair to the right of the doorway.

Ruby stood up and grabbed Obermeier by the tie and threw him against the desk. He kicked the door shut with the heel of his shoe.

"Good morning, Carl. You need to hire better help. I was supposed to have been your Patsy, but you needed better than Freddie to take care of me."

"Oh, God! Oh, sweet Jesus!"

Rick slapped him across the mouth.

"Don't be profane, Carl, you're a Jew. Leave the blasphemy to the goyim."

He grabbed Obermeier by the scruff of the neck and lifted him three inches into the air.

"You have exactly thirty seconds to come clean with me or I start pouring the gasoline down your throat and then I'll start looking for matches."

He heard the sound of leaking and then felt the trickle of wetness on his shoe. Rick threw Obermeier into his seat and looked with contempt at the spreading stain down the front of the man's pants.

"Talk!" Rick hissed through clenched teeth.

"Are you insane?" Obermeier managed to convey authority despite his very evident and reasonable fear for his life, "Don't you realize who I am? Irene has probably already called security. I'll have you shot before you get out the door."

"Then I'll go out the way I came in."

Rick jerked a thumb toward the open window as the curtain blew gently in the morning breeze.

"Even if you do get away, I have connections. East and West. You'll never get away with it."

"I don't intend to, Carl. However, I'll have the satisfaction of taking you down first."

Rick reached for the first can of gasoline and pulled the stopper loose. He lifted the canister and began pouring it out over Obermeier's head.

"Oh God! I'll talk." Obermeier choked on the gasoline dripping into his mouth and stinging his eyes. "I'll tell you everything."

"That's more like it."

Rick set the canister back down on the desk. He picked a pack of Camel's off the desk and offered it to Obermeier.

"Care for a smoke?"

Obermeier cringed as he started to soil his pants.

"No? Probably a good move on your part. Start talking, Carl. I'd like to be finished with you before Irene brings in your coffee and the morning paper."

Obermeier cleared his throat and tried to calm his racing nerves.

"Blackie got to be a problem for the studio. The scandal sheets were starting to hear rumors about him. Not the normal stuff either. Weird crap. The sort of stories that could sink the studio. My father spoke to him a few times, but it didn't do any good so he told me to replace him. My father wasn't aware that Champlain-Blackie was a copyright claimant. He never would have agreed to a production company run by the star and screen-writer sharing copyright control over the pictures with Monorail. J. C. was fine with replacing him. Hell, she would have been ecstatic, but there was the legal problem."

"We were pretty sure that the kids who watch this junk wouldn't have noticed. We'd just tell them the next actor was Tulsa's brother and after a week or two they wouldn't even remember what Blackie looked like. The problem was how to get rid of Blackie."

"So you did the smart thing, you let the writer script his exit. Is that it?"

Obermeier nodded, "How did you figure that out?"

Rick shrugged. "Certain phrases she kept using. It began to sound like it was a story after awhile instead of real life. Hollywood never can get dialogue right. Even Aunt Minnie knows from corn. The real tip-off was when we were talking to the cops after the old man and his goon were dead. She knew Gilbert picked me up outside Blackie's apartment. I never told her that. Everyone was so sure I was a dumb cluck that they started getting sloppy."

Obermeier grimaced. "Things got complicated. The plan was to lay the blame on Connelly. He was a blackmailer. He tried putting the squeeze on Blackie first. Blackie came to talk to me and warned J. C. about it. Then she heard from Connelly. That's when she came to me with the idea of pinning it on the old man since he was a bum already."

Rick nodded. "Couldn't ask for a better snake than that old man. Where did I fit in?"

"We needed a patsy. Nothing personal, but we needed a snoop…prefer-ably from out of town…who could drive everyone down the wrong avenue and then bring them all safely home at just the right time."

Rick nodded again. "And if I happened to get bumped off along the way, no harm done."

"Occupational hazard, Mr. Ruby. It comes with the territory."

"That it does, Carl, only I never even had a chance, did I? There's no way you were going to let me go with those two suitcases, was there?"

"Retrieving the suitcases was Freddie's job, but I swear killing you wasn't part of the plan. He was supposed to get the money back and rough you up a little. Scare you bad enough to get on that plane and go home. We couldn't have another murder on our hands or someone would start asking questions. It was pushing it with three bodies already. Four was too great a risk."

"Glad to know you're not a gambling man, Carl. What about Freddie? I thought he worked for the old lady…or was she in on the action, too?"

"Mrs. Finster was innocent…as far as all of this was concerned. Freddie and Gilbert were employed by Connelly. They came with him from Tulsa. It didn't take much for J. C. to convince them that they could profitably serve two masters."

"Looked like the convincing got her roughed up a bit."

"Men like Gilbert and Freddie generally have violent streaks and I'm afraid Connelly could not control them as well as he liked to think. We put Freddie in with the old lady to help keep tabs on her and make sure she wasn't going to make trouble for us. J. C. liked the old lady, but she wasn't sure how much she could trust her to be honest."

Rick laughed. "As if either of you know anything about trust or honesty."

"One can appreciate qualities one does not possess, Mr. Ruby."

"Very eloquently put, Carl. I guess that just about covers it."

Obermeier looked nervous, "What now?"

Rick shrugged, "Now you go through everything you just told me again only this time with Irene taking notes."

Obermeier looked at him puzzled.

"A memo to your Dad. I figure he'll be more likely to give you what you deserve than the police…oh and uh, so there's no hard feelings with the firm, I'll be taking my usual fee and leaving the rest of the money in the two suitcases behind. I always play fair, Carl. It's good for business and your health. A pity you never learned that lesson. One way or another, if you're dishonest in this world, you can bet you'll end up getting burned."

Joanna was packing when Rick reached her bungalow.

"Going somewhere, J. C.?"

She looked up at him while shoving another pile of clothes into the suitcase. Her eye was still badly bruised. She hadn't bothered with makeup and looked all the worse for it.

"You idiot." She sounded surprisingly calm as she stared at him. "You loused everything up royally, didn't you?"

"Real life isn't like one of your scripts, J. C. People get hurt. They do unexpected things. You can't plan out real life like a story. There are too many variables for one of your plots to ever play out as well as it does on paper."

"Thanks for the tip. Next time I'll remember not to let hired help do the job for me."

She pulled her hand from the suitcase. She aimed the tiny revolver at Rick and pulled the trigger.

He ducked to one side and the bullet grazed his shoulder. He reached across the desk and twisted her arm roughly until the revolver dropped from her hand. He backhanded her hard across the face and she fell down into the cushioned chair behind the desk.

"That's a woman's gun, J. C. You've got to hit something vital with that toy if you want to stop somebody in their tracks."

He grabbed the revolver and shoved it into his pants pocket.

"I see that Carl called you after I left him. I'm glad to see that he did the gentlemanly thing under the circumstances."

"No," she shook her head, "Irene called me. Carl did the cowardly thing and hung himself in his office once you left."

Rick smiled, "If this is the scene where I'm supposed to feel bad for Carl, you've misunderstood my character entirely. I gave him a chance at the only justice he merited. He chose his own path. I didn't tie the noose for him."

"You might as well have. Why did you have to stick your nose in everything? So Freddie was an idiot. He deserved to die if he couldn't follow orders. You could have taken the money and gone back to New York and everything would have turned out just fine."

"Oh sure, that would have been swell. That is until Carl had to explain to his father about that little irregularity in the accounting books. And then I would have had to deal with some cement shoes in the Hudson Bay and I'll be perfectly honest with you, I think I would look terrible and feel worse with cement shoes on my feet and seaweed in my mouth…so really, sweetheart, I didn't have much of a choice but to stick my nose into the mess you made."

"There wouldn't have been a trail to follow. Carl and I were planning on going to South America to start over with a new life…under new names. Now I'll be going by myself it seems."

"Sorry, sweetheart, still not buying it. You didn't love Carl any more than you loved any man. He was just another rung on the ladder for you, that's all. Carl thought the plan was to replace Blackie with another actor. Tulsa's brother was how you scripted it…at least that's what he told me. You may have been planning to go to South America all along, but it wasn't with Carl. Now tell me…was the cap gun meant for him all along? You really couldn't leave a partner-in-crime hanging around, now could you?"

She laughed for a second.

"I misjudged your intelligence, Ruby."

"Yeah, it's the face and the red hair. Everybody makes that mistake. I need to figure out how to make that pay. The only thing is now I can't let you go to South America."

"I don't have to go alone, Rick."

She looked at him and the look in her eyes actually made it seem like she meant it. That's what scared him.

"The thing with you, sweetheart, is that I'd have to keep waiting for that knife in my back while I slept. Girls like you are poison. Mama was right about that at least."

She reached forward and grabbed him by the lapels of his coat and pulled him close and kissed him roughly on the mouth. After a second, the kiss turned silky smooth like milk flowing from a cup. Rick felt himself stiffen with desire.

"Do you always listen to Mama when it comes to girls, Rick?"

"Honestly? Never. Mama wasn't trying to get laid. She was another one who completely misjudged my character."

Joanna laughed. "You're cute, you know that? I'm sorry I never had the pleasure, Mr. Ruby, but I know better than to trust a redhead. That's why I can't trust you with this."

Her lady's revolver was back in her hand. She was good, he hadn't even felt her hand in his pants pocket. That was talent.

"Something vital, I believe you said."

"Don't be stupid, Joanna, you'll never get away with it."

"I know," she said and placed the gun to her temple and pulled the trigger.

The sound reverberated in his mind long after the ugly visuals faded away into the blackness. It had finished at last.

It was just before four in the afternoon when Rick reached the bus terminal.

He took out the cash he had crumpled up in his pocket. What was left of his fee would just about cover a bus back to New York.

The man in the ticket booth looked at him through eyes squinting over a pair of bifocals.

"You from New York, Mister?"

"That's right."

"You don't seem too happy to be going back."

Rick grinned for a minute as he thought about that.

"I guess you could say I came out here in style. Private plane. Nice car. The works. Now it's back to the real world."

"Yeah, just another dreamer. I see your type all the time. You come out to Hollywood in search of your dreams and then you wake up broke and head back home brokenhearted. If you ask me the smart ones never dream in the first place."

"You gotta dream, friend, no matter where you're from. Without your dreams, you're just left with the harsh reality that this life is just a series of avenues that always wind up in a dead end."

"Ain't that the truth?" The little man nodded behind his bifocals. "All the same, you're better off not taking any chances in life. The higher you climb, the harder you fall. You know what I mean, Mister?"

Rick nodded, "I do. I do, indeed. There's always an empty swimming pool just waiting for you somewhere."

The little man squinted and wrinkled his nose to push his bifocals back into place. This time he just looked at Rick and didn't say another word.

The End

PAYING OLD DEBTS

This story was great fun to write because Rick Ruby is the latest iteration of that hardboiled knight errant who started in the pulps as Sam Spade and Philip Marlowe and made it to the airwaves as Johnny Dollar and Richard Diamond before crossing to television as Peter Gunn. For me, a very personal debt is owed first and foremost to Blake Edwards (1922-2010). Without his work as an inspiration, I would never have wanted to become a writer.

Edwards is best-remembered for The Pink Panther series or films like *Breakfast at Tiffany's, Days of Wine and Roses, The Great Race, "10," S.O.B.,* and *Victor/Victoria*. His broad body of work as a writer-producer-director spanned seven decades and encompassed radio, television, film, and theater. During his years in radio, he wrote for the long-running *Yours Truly, Johnny Dollar* (and later brought the character to television in an unsold TV pilot in 1962) and created, wrote and directed *Richard Diamond, Private Detective*. When Diamond later made a successful transition to television without him, Edwards created, produced, wrote and directed *Peter Gunn*. He remade many of his old *Diamond* radio scripts for the *Gunn* TV series. Edwards loved the character so much that he brought him back for a 1967 feature film and a 1989 TV-movie. During the final years of his life, Edwards was working diligently at developing yet another revival of the property.

What does all of this have to do with Rick Ruby, you ask? For me, everything. Rick Ruby is my chance to play in the same field and repay some old debts to the masters of the genre that inspired me: Hammett, Chandler, Ross Macdonald, and most especially, Blake Edwards. Their work gave me something to identify with and strive for as well as providing escapism when I was a kid growing up in the 1970s. While other kids my age were reading The Hardy Boys or Encyclopedia Brown, I was trying to figure out what a gunsel was in *The Maltese Falcon*.

The character of Tulsa Blackie isn't based on any particular cowboy star. The name is derived from Blake Edwards' nickname of Blackie and certain aspects of the character's back-story (including the incident of diving head-first into an empty swimming pool) are embellished versions of incidents that occurred in Edwards' actual life. Blake Edwards was a native of Tulsa, Oklahoma. The son of Donald and Lillian Crump. Lillian did move to Hollywood after divorcing her first husband and married a production manager named Jack McEdward whose father was known as J. Gordon Edwards (a legendary silent film director who made numerous films with silent film vamp, Theda Bara). William Blake Crump (as he was christened at birth) grew up in the home of his spinster aunts in Tulsa until he was high school age and moved to Beverly Hills, where his stepfather adopted him.

Rod Cameron was the closest model for Tulsa Blackie in as much as he started out as a double for Fred MacMurray at Paramount before signing on as a star of B-movies for Monogram Pictures. Among the first of which were the cowboy films, *Panhandle* and *Stampede*. Before Monogram became Allied Artists, they really did pioneer the use of production companies owned by producers and writers who bankrolled their own pictures in exchange for partial ownership. It was a practice that grew commonplace once the studio system collapsed in the late 1950s. The long-running detective series, *The Falcon* was the series that switched stars and explained it away as having the character's brother take over as the titular hero.

J. C. Champlain shares two real-life inspirations. The first was Leigh Brackett, one of the first women screenwriters who distinguished herself writing *The Big Sleep* and went on to write such classics as *Rio Bravo* and *The Empire Strikes Back*. Ms. Brackett found that most executives and producers assumed she was a man in her early days in Hollywood. Her novel, *No Good From a Corpse,* remains one of the lost classics of hardboiled detective fiction and led to her getting the assignment from Howard Hawks to adapt Raymond Chandler's first Philip Marlowe novel to the big screen.

Champlain's other inspiration was J. C. Champion. John C. Champion was the son of a Bank of America president who became a screenwriter and producer starting at Monogram Pictures. His writing and producing partner was a friend from Beverly Hills High named Blake Edwards. Their company, Champion-Edwards was one of the first of the new breed of production companies that became common place in the last half-century of Hollywood. Their first efforts as writer-producers were the aforementioned Rod Cameron westerns.

Carl Obermeier, Jr. owes his debt of inspiration to Carl Laemmle, Jr. whose father founded Universal Pictures. The younger Laemmle is the man who greenlit the classic Universal Horrors of the 1930s starring Bela

Lugosi and Boris Karloff that did so much to shape 20th Century pop culture. "Junior" Laemmle was one of several sons of studio executives who had to bear the witty riposte, "The Son Also Rises" in reference to the nepotism that was rampant in the Golden Age of Hollywood.

The references to Cole Porter's song, "Easy to Love" and the board game Monopoly are historically accurate for the time frame. Both song and board game captured the imaginations of many during the late 1930s. The references to Prohibition and the transition from silent movies to talkies as well as mention of silent era cowboy star Tom Mix (who, like my fictional Tulsa Blackie, always played himself and never a "character") are also in keeping with what would have been the common memories of most adults in the 1930s.

Thank you to Ron Fortier for his friendship, support, and encouragement to contribute a story to Airship 27. It was a long time coming, Ron. I hope it was worth it. Rick Ruby is a great character, and I'm thrilled to be part of the team bringing him to life. Hopefully somewhere there's a kid reading this book who is inspired to dig back and find the roots of the genre and better still, to sit down at his laptop and start his own story. In the end, we're all repaying old debts. That's what storytelling is all about.

WILLIAM PATRICK MAYNARD was authorized to continue Sax Rohmer's Fu Manchu thrillers beginning with **The Terror of Fu Manchu** *(2009; Black Coat Press). A sequel,* **The Destiny of Fu Manchu** *is due for publication in April 2012. Also forthcoming is a collection of short stories featuring an original Edwardian detective,* **The Occult Case Book of Shankar Hardwicke** *and an original hardboiled detective novel,* **Lawhead**. *His short fiction has been published in Gaslight Grotesque (2009; EDGE Publishing), Tales of the Shadowmen: Grand Guignol (2009; Black Coat Press), and Les Compagnons de L'ombre, Tome 6 (2010; Riviere Blanche). He contributes weekly articles to the website, The Black Gate and had previously done the same for The Cimmerian. His articles have also been published in* **Blood 'n' Thunder**, *Van Helsing's Journal, and by The Peter Sellers Appreciation Society. He was nominated for a Pulp Factory Award for Best Pulp Novel for* **The Terror of Fu Manchu** *and he was nominated for a Rondo Award for an article in Van Helsing's Journal. He makes his home in Northeast Ohio with his wife and family.*

Die Giftige Lilie

By Sean Taylor

The woman's accent was just German enough to get his attention, all dripping with sexy gutturals and thick vowels, just exotic enough to trick a man's ears into thinking he was having a drink with Marlene Dietrich instead of some two-bit nightclub singer in a no-account New York dive like Belle's. But the comparison stopped cold at the woman's voice. She was attractive, of course, but lacked the sex appeal that would have brought sell-out crowds to the local bijou. Her skin was pale and almost sickly, and her figure—while a far sight better than that of the average woman with a nice apartment and radio in her living room—well, it was never going to get her silhouette painted on a playbill. But her eyes, her dark eyes that threatened to go solid black in just the right light, those were something special, and it was those eyes that had convinced him to listen to her story in the first place.

"So listen, honey," he said, tapping a Camel from a pack of cigarettes then slipping it back inside his coat pocket.

"Gerta," she said.

"Right. Gerta Stein. You said that." He smiled and nodded as he lit the Camel. "So, what's all this noise about your uncle?"

She shifted her weight in her seat, and he pretended to be gentleman enough not to overtly notice the way her dress slipped off the side of her thigh. "I think he's in trouble, Mr. Ruby. I think he's in the kind of trouble could get him killed."

"What kind of trouble is that, honey?"

"My Uncle Oskar, he's a scientist, a chemist who works on weapons development. Only, he's not very happy with the direction our government has taken, and he's looking for an opportunity to seek sanctuary here in your United States."

"Sounds like a smart man."

"He's very smart, Mr. Ruby." There went those legs again, uncrossing and then stacking one on top of the other in the opposite manner. Rick didn't pretend as well this time. Still, she either didn't notice or didn't seem to mind. "He is in New York with a group of scientists and officials for some kind of conference, and he's staying at the Grand Hotel."

"Nice place. Ritzy. Expensive."

"Yes. The Nazis spare no expense to keep their war makers pliable and complacent, Mr. Ruby."

He stopped her by raising his index finger between them.

"If I'm going to help you, honey," he said, intentionally not watching the swing of her legs, "then we're going to have to get one thing straight. My friends call me Rick. Only the bankers, cops, and jealous boyfriends call me Mr. Ruby. Okay?"

"Then I'd prefer you call me Gerta as well."

"Sure thing, honey." He smiled. "So, Gerta, tell me more about your Uncle Oskar."

She stifled a shudder and continued. "Word has gotten out among his companions that he wants to stay and become a United States citizen, and I overheard several of the party officials traveling with him plotting to have him either killed or beaten and forced back to Germany."

Rick finished the last of his Camel, then tapped another out of the pack. "Cigarette?" he offered.

Gerta shook her head. "Well, Mr. Ruby?"

Rick raised his index finger again.

"I'm sorry. Rick?"

"That's better, honey." He lit the second Camel and took a long drag, sucked it into his lungs and then blew it out his nose. "Two things. One, seems to me there are other channels in place for handling this kind of noise, official government channels who would be tripping over themselves to get a Nazi scientist here on the U.S. payroll."

"German scientist, Rick."

"What?"

He's a German scientist, not a Nazi. We do not all support the party even though we may still love our homeland. One can do more to effect change from within that from without."

"Ah. Yes. Sorry."

She smiled.

He took the gesture as a signal to keep going. "Anyway, I'd think you'd have more luck finding the proper channels to arrange for his escape from his companions."

"We don't have time to find them out, Mr. Ruby. Even now it may already be too late."

Rick reached across the table for her hand, hoping to calm her display. "Which brings me to my second point, and I hate to sound so mercenary, but I do require a week's expenses up front and a per diem after that. Will you be able to cover my financial necessities for this case if I agree to take it on?"

Gerta bit down on her bottom lip, opened her eyes wide and black, and waved her leg again. Rick almost told her he could give her a discounted rate, but that empty feeling in his pockets reminded him that louse or not, he still had bills to pay. Besides, if she couldn't cover his costs, he could at least introduce her to Mac and let the coppers handle it for her. Either way, she'd get the help she needed.

She sniffled loudly and rested her hands, folded together, in her narrow lap.

He started to speak, but thought better of it and simply let his smile stretch into a sort of, he hoped, silly grin.

Gerta uncrossed her legs and leaned forward, reaching for her handbag sitting on the floor at her thin, pale feet, even through the stockings. When she sat up again, she held her bag in her lap and one hand had disappeared inside.

Rick tried not to raise his gaze to follow the hand inside the black leather.

"Will this do, Rick?" she asked as she placed a neatly bound stack of twenty dollar bills on the table between them. "My family has more than sufficient resources to pay for your services, I assure you."

Rick nodded. "That's a good start, honey."

Damn, there went those pale legs again, re-crossing back to the way they had been initially. She noticed him admiring them. "The payment stops at money, Mr. Ruby, no matter how much you may like what you see. I may be desperate for your help, but –"

"It's not like that, honey. I can enjoy the stilts without needing to try 'em out myself, I assure you. I'd never take advantage of a woman, no matter how vulnerable she might be. I'm the good guy, remember?"

As he said it, he picked up the money and shuffled through it. Thick, he thought. Far more than enough to cover the first week's expenses. Maybe enough for the first two, not that the case would need two weeks, he figured.

"But not a complete good Samaritan, I see," she said with a friendly smirk.

"Got to pay the room and board, honey. They don't give out these licenses for free."

The room grew quiet, and everyone was suddenly looking at them. No, he realized, not at them but through them.

He turned to follow the stares.

All the way to the stage.

A slender shadow of black curves stood poured into a shiny silver dress that flowed down to two stocking-clad legs perched atop matching silver shoes. Then the shadow opened up to reveal a smile white enough to hit the room like a spotlight.

Evelyn Johnson had taken the stage.

And she was staring at him, her eyes locked onto his, ignoring the pale, dark-eyed German woman seated beside him.

"This is for everyone helping to keep Belle's alive, one drink at a time," she said, then the band kicked into "Riffin' the Scotch."

"She seems to know you," Gerta said.

"We… have a history."

"I imagine you have a history with more women that you let any of them know."

"A gentleman never discusses past loves."

"A gentleman?"

She was bouncing those damn legs again and staring at him with those eyes so black he couldn't see the light reflect back at him.

"As much a gentleman as my upbringing will allow me to be," he said.

She reached across the table to take his hand, then cocooned it between both of her own. "Thank you, Rick. You'll never know what this means to me. I couldn't live with myself if anything happened to him."

Rick wasn't looking, but he felt Evelyn's eyes boring into him.

"Think nothing of it, honey. It's what I'm trained to do."

Gerta squeezed his hand. "It looks to me like your history thinks you have a present tense."

"Yeah, well…"

"As I said, Rick, I do not intend to become part of your history, so it's really none of my business." She let go of his hand. "But I do admit that her jealousy gives me a delightful feeling I haven't felt in a while."

"…I lost me a cheatin' man," Evelyn sang with the thick syrup of her voice. "And got a no-count liar…"

Rick felt his throat constrict and fill with something he tried to tell himself didn't taste like guilt. Evelyn knew they weren't a regular item, and that he didn't expect any more of her than he wanted her to expect of him. Besides, with society being what it was, if word got out about their occasional crossing of the racial divide, chances are that they'd both be strung up—at least figuratively—by the good citizens of New York. And Rick liked having his figurative neck in place just as much as his literal one.

"So let's get out of here, honey, and go meet this uncle of yours."

The last thing he heard before hitting the door was Evelyn's voice cracking with intentional pretense, "…Swapped the old one for a new one, now the new one's breakin' my heart…"

Walking the human clutter of Oak Street reminded Rick of both the beauty and the foulness of New York. Breadlines shuddered hungry on one corner while top hats and shiny gowns packed the theaters to laugh at Cary Grant and Katherine Hepburn's staged pratfalls and one-liners in *Bringing Up Baby* less than a block away. Torn somewhere between poverty and luxury, New York was as schizophrenic a lady as he'd ever known, and difficult both to hold any long-term affection for and avoid regularly falling in love with like a schoolboy with a crush on an alluring young school teacher.

"Your New York City is a beautiful city," Gerta said, her heels click-clacking on the sidewalk.

"She's a fickle place," he mumbled.

"Not grand and glorious like my own Hamburg, of course, but lovely like a young woman, not a stately lady. Evidence of her need to grow up is all around, but the maturing features are still beautiful nevertheless."

"You never told me you had the heart of a poet, honey."

"I…" she started, and he could almost hear her throat try to block the words. "I get sentimental about my home. It wasn't always a *Gau* for the Nazis, Mr. Ruby. There was a time when it was a place to respect our history and not try to enforce the party's understanding of the future."

He said nothing, and instead grabbed the pack of Camels from his coat pocket and felt the wind blow through his thick red hair. With all the hats men seemed to find fashionable, he found that he could stand out better without one. Of course, when he needed to hide in a crowd, there were plenty of fedoras to be had for a modest price. He tapped out a cigarette and offered one to Gerta. She declined.

"I'm not here to judge, honey." Rick lit the Camel and sucked a thick tarry stretch of smoke into his lungs. "We all have our sins to account for."

"I assure you, Mr. Ruby. The party has more than a few small sins to account for. The bastards pretend to be about the German workers, but—"

She stifled a choking cough. "I'm sorry. After how the party has treated my uncle, I tend to lose my temper when I think about them."

"Like I said, I'm not here to judge." He cocked his head to the side and grinned, hoping more for charm than goofiness. "Say, you speak English like a pro. What gives?"

"I sing," she said.

"I know. I've caught your act. Not bad."

"Thank you, Rick."

"That doesn't completely answer my question."

She ran her fingers through her hair, tucking it behind her ear. "I have lived in the United States for several years. Before my manager booked me into New York, I used to perform in San Francisco, Carson City and Denver. It was his idea to move me to the east coast in hopes of bigger crowds and better money."

"Aw," Rick mumbled more than said. "The filthy lucre."

"Says the man who demanded a week's pay up front."

"Never claimed to be free of the root of all evil, doll."

"Please, it's Gerta."

"Okay. Gerta." Rick caught a whiff of fish and knew they were getting near the markets. "Still, not much of an accent at all."

"I tend to pick up accents of the people I'm around, I'm afraid. You should hear me when after my uncle visits. I can almost taste the thick German that creeps back in. And let me tell you, Rick, the only time an American wants to hear German is in the cinema or from the mouth of a female crooner in a slinky gown."

"Well, can't say that I disagree terribly, honey."

"You haven't met the right Germans then, Rick."

Rick smiled and glanced in her eyes just long enough to see the doors close there.

"But don't get ideas."

"No ma'am," he said. "Best behavior."

"It's around the next block, Mr. Ruby."

Rick shook his head and took another long drag on the cigarette to get the fish smell out of his nose. "Let's not go back to that noise, Gerta. I thought we were getting to be friends."

She smiled but said nothing.

"Hope you don't keep your windows open, honey."

Gerta looked at him, scrunched her eyes in thought, then nodded. "Oh. The smell. No. We don't get it much on the other side of the block. The wind ignores us, so the smell never seems to reach my windows."

"Thank heaven for small favors," Rick muttered mostly as an excuse to keep talking.

"And for large ones, Rick." Gerta slowed and turned to face him. Those black eyes probed him and came up full of information, he was sure. "Like finding you to help my Uncle Oskar."

"Don't make me out to be a saint, honey." Rick tightened his lock on her arm and brought her heels back up to speed on the sidewalk. "Because I'm not ready to die for anybody's faith in me, and those who think too highly of me usually end up pretty disappointed."

Gerta grinned and laughed, then stifled the sound. "You're too hard on yourself, Rick. No man or woman knows he or she is a saint. It's only the hindsight of history that reveals the truth about them." Her hand stretched out, each finger trying to escape the confines of its neighbor, then they rested again across his knuckles. "You may surprise yourself set."

"And half of New York, I'm certain."

She smiled, then stopped then at a set of eight stone steps. "We're here. My temporary home."

"Thought you said he was staying at the Grand."

"He is. But surely you didn't think we would meet him there with all his—"

Rick stopped her cold. Pressed his lips against hers then shoved them both against the stone railing that lead up the steps. She resisted the intrusion for a moment, then relented and stopped squirming in his grip, and Rick felt her breath push her chest against him in a slow, steady, deliberate rhythm that felt like the band at Belle's.

He watched as the blue sedan cleared the corner and disappeared.

Then he returned to the kiss, gave it a few more seconds just for the hell of it, and finally released both her arms and lips.

For a moment, Gerta stood shakily on the steps until she braced herself on the railing with her left hand. Then with her right, she swung back and let it go toward Rick's face.

He smiled and caught the delicate wrist before she connected with his cheek, then said, "They've been following us since the moment we stepped out of Belle's. I needed a reason to slow down and let them pass and to get a good look at them as they did. Two men, both blonde, one's tall enough to bump his head on the top of the car. Ring any bells?"

"You may let go of my arm at any time, Mr. Ruby."

"Now let's not start that Mr. Ruby noise again, honey. I told you, it was just a diversion to let them pass."

"And the extra time after they did so?"

"Oh. You noticed that."

"I most certainly did."

"Well, that was for you. You seemed to be enjoying it, so I—"

Slap!

Her left hand all but leapt from the railing and did its damndest to leave a calling card on his face. He felt the Camel dive from his hand.

He let go of her arm and took a step back. "Ouch."

"I'm left-handed, Rick. And whether I enjoyed it or not, my embraces are not part of your daily fee, I recall."

"Don't get your skirt ruffled, doll. I assure you I meant nothing by it." He grinned and waited for her to return the feeling. When she didn't, he continued, "So, Gerta, do you know of any German treetops hanging around your uncle?"

"German treetops?" She looked at him flatly, then smiled. "Ah, the tall men. I do find your way of speaking both refreshing and exasperating, Rick."

"So we're back to Rick now?"

"Well, as you said, nothing was meant by the gesture."

Rick said nothing.

"Don't look so hurt, Rick."

"Well, they know we're here and most likely why we're here, so I guess we might as well get moving."

Gerta's face grew pale and skeletal. "Do you suppose I've put him in danger just bringing you here, Rick?"

Rick grabbed her hand and pulled her up the steps toward the doors. "Let's worry about that when the time comes, honey. Right now, let's get Uncle Oskar to somewhere safe."

Once inside, Gerta guided Rick to the elevators, but he stopped her and motioned toward the stairs instead, the stairs in the back. After three flights as quietly as they could walk, even making Gerta take the dirty steps in stocking feet, Rick cracked open the door and peeked into the hallway.

Sure enough, a German soldier leaned against the wall with a clear view of the elevator cage.

Rick closed the door and whispered. "Okay, honey, it's time to take a walk and make it count."

"I'm afraid I don't understand, Rick."

"Don't get innocent on me now, Gerta. If we're going to get your uncle somewhere safe, I need to know that soldier-boy there is watching you, not me."

"Ah. I understand."

"Good girl. Now slip those high-heeled click-clackers back on and put those stilts of yours to good use."

"You don't give up, do you, Rick?" she breathed at him.

"Not for me this time, baby. Promise."

She grinned. "Methinks you doth protest too much."

"So the lady knows her Shakespeare." He motioned toward the door. "We'll trade books later. For now, let's go get your uncle."

As she brushed past him and gripped the doorknob, she leaned toward him, almost resting her chin on his shoulder. "I did enjoy it, Rick."

"I—"

"But don't consider that an invitation for an encore, Mr. Ruby."

"Whatever you say, baby."

"Gerta."

"Right."

He stepped back into the shadows of the stairwell as she swung open the door and swished into the hallway. He let the door hit the frame enough to clank but not far enough to click shut. Then he pushed it open just wide enough to see the straight black seam of Gerta's stockings sashay past the soldier.

She nodded at the soldier as she passed, and he said "Guten Tag, Fraulein."

She responded in German, and Rick wished he had learned the language. But it wasn't much and the important part of the conversation was in the tone, not the words. She had hooked her fish, and that was all that mattered, and with each step away from him, she pulled the barb in farther. Rick kept one eye on the soldier as he tilted his head after her for a better angle and one eye on her legs himself.

"Damn my time," he muttered, and he pushed the door open quietly and stepped into the hallway. Germany's finest never had a chance. In three wide steps, Rick had cleared the distance between them and sent him to dreamland with the butt of his Colt .38. No sooner had the young man hit the floor than Gerta stopped and began to click her heel on the marble floor.

"Is he… dead?"

"Not this time. He'll live to plague the free world again, honey. But not your uncle."

"This way," she motioned to a door three rooms down the hallway. "Room 347."

Rick nodded. "You knock, but let me go in first. If they've got a boy out here, they could just as well have one inside."

She gave him a worried smile and nodded once.

Then she walked to the door, knocked three times and called out, "Uncle Oskar. It's me, Gerta. I'm back."

No one answered.

Rick nodded at Gerta. "Say hello."

"Uncle Oskar, it's just me. I wanted to invite you to my show tonight."

The door cracked open. Rick backed away out of view. "Your uncle is sleeping, Fraulein Stein. You may leave the tickets with me."

Rick thought for a moment that it was odd the German would be speaking English, but he had no time to wonder about it in depth, because Gerta pushed open the door all the way.

"I need to see him, and I am to believe this is a free country."

The door opened to darkness, the only light, the glint of steel thanks to the hallway chandeliers.

"Gerta!" came a voice from inside the room.

In a flash, Rick dove from his hiding place at the edge of the door, sending both himself and Gerta onto the floor. Just as fast the .38 was aimed at the shadow in the doorway. Before he could fire, though, a loud clang resonated from within the room, and the shadow melted onto the floor.

"Are you okay, my flower?" said the same voice from a moment before.

"You may get up off me, Rick. I believe we're safe now."

Rick realized that in the dive, he had managed to roll Gerta completely onto her back and use his own body as a shield, with the exception of one of his knees planted firmly between her own. "Anything you say, honey."

As he pushed up to his feet, he took a moment to give Uncle Oskar a once-over, then a twice-over. Probably pushing his mid-50s. Gray in all the ways that make a man look older than he actually is. Unkempt, and he obviously didn't rate his appearance high on his list of priorities. He fit every stereotype Rick had imagined.

"Thank you for distracting him, Gerta." Uncle Oskar returned the favor and gave Rick a clearly suspicious examination. "You and your... friend."

"This..." she began, then cut her eyes at Rick. "This gentleman is a private detective in my employ, Uncle. I hired him because I was worried about you."

When Rick was securely standing, he reached for Gerta's hand to help her up as well. "Your niece is concerned that you're being strong-armed and believes you might want to stay here in the land of the free and the home of the brave."

Uncle Oskar leaned into the hallway and checked both directions. "The other soldier?"

"He's taking a nap."

"Gerta is correct, Mr. Ruby."

"We can work out the details later, but for now, let's get you somewhere safe, both of you."

"**L**isten, Edie, honey," Rick said as he tried to swallow a huge bite of his secretary's apple pie.

"Oh no, Rick Ruby. Not for all the charm in that insincere lump you call a heart." The normally sweet voice of Edie Rose Adams threatened to tip the scales into an actual yell. But just barely. If Edie was anything, she was all decorum and self-control.

He was counting on it.

She didn't let him down.

"You cannot use my suite as a safe house for a Nazi scientist and a night-club singer." She turned to Gerta. "No offense."

Gerta grinned. "None taken."

"You're my best bet for keeping them safe, honey."

"Don't honey me, Rick."

"C'mon, doll. Uncle Oskar here wants to become a free man, a citizen of the U.S.A."

Edie wrapped her arms over her chest with a loud humph.

"What's it going to cost me?"

"Don't mind us," Gerta said. "We promise you'll never know we're here."

"It's not that," Edie said, tossing a thick fluff of hair back over her ear. "It's who else might know that you're here. And after the last bullet I took for you, Rick, I don't have taking another one on my Christmas list."

"Nobody knows, honey. I promise."

"Nobody knew last time."

"I—"

"In spite of your promise last time too."

"Edie, Edie, Edie…" Rick started, then saw the Bible she had left on the kitchen counter. Decorum and self-control indeed. Especially to read all that jazz in the kitchen. "What would Jesus do?"

Edie stopped, her breath seemed to stick in her throat. "You didn't read it, did you?"

"Just enough."

"Now you start to listen to me?"

"I ain't puttin' in for sainthood, honey, but I'll tell you what. You do me this favor, and I'll actually go down to the mission with you this week."

Edie looked at the old man and the female crooner. A little jealously, Rick thought, when she took a few extra seconds to take in Gerta. But that was okay. Sometimes a man had to keep the women in his life playing against each other to get the results he needed. And sometimes to get the results he wanted, whether he needed them or not.

"Well?"

"I'm thinking."

He leaned in and placed a tender kiss on her cheek. "Promise. Scout's honor. Nothing's gonna happen this time."

"Damn it, Rick."

"Watch that language, honey," Rick laughed.

"You bring out the worst in me, Rick Ruby."

"So you'll do it?"

Edie stared at the floor. "Yes. I'll do it. But so help me if you try to get out of the meeting at the mission, I'll never speak to you again, and you can start looking for a new secretary."

"You're a saint, honey."

"Thank you," said Gerta.

"Yes, thank you for your hospitality, Miss Adams," said Uncle Oskar.

"You have to die to be a saint, Rick."

"Oh."

Edie shook her head. "Would you like some tea?" she asked her new guests.

"Do you have scotch?" asked Uncle Oskar.

Edie shot Rick a glance. Rick smiled.

"No, sir," she said emphatically. "I do not keep any alcohol at home, Mr. Stein."

Rick laughed as he headed for the door. "You'll be safe here, and Edie will take good care of you."

Gerta had taken a seat on Edie's sofa and was bouncing those damn legs again. He tried not to linger, but stayed just long enough for Edie to notice.

"Don't you have somewhere to be, boss?"

"Yes, ma'am, I do." He winked at Edie. "You're the best, honey. Never forget that."

"Pride is a sin, Rick," she said, then added with a whisper. "Just like lust."

"Yeah, I guess I need to get a move on."

Edie's voice dropped even softer. "Rick?"

"Yeah, honey?"

"Please be careful. I worry about you."

Good ol' Mac, Rick thought, as he crouched in the shadows behind the Wellington Fish Co. warehouse. The place stunk to high-heaven, and not just because of the wet meat in the boxes. He could take the odor of fish over the odor of Nazis and sympathizers any day, especially the kind who put dames like Gerta on their hit lists.

Thank God he still had a friend or two with a badge. It saved hours of hoofing it and miles of leg work.

Even after five years on the force himself, the department by and large had little love for him. Sure, he had a damn good reason for quitting and fading away into a drunken stupor—God rest Greer Lawson's soul—and it hadn't even been his idea in the first place to come out of the gutter and get his P.I. license, but none of that seemed to matter to bucks who still wore the blue and carried the badge. They just didn't like private dicks like him getting in the way of the justice machine.

Mostly because without all the hoops to jump through, he could get the job done quicker and easier, though he might have to bend the letter of the law occasionally.

Still, he did have a few friends on the force, as long as he didn't mind not using more than one hand to count them. And Mac had come through with flying colors this time, tracking down the license plate with the county, and given him the address down at the docks.

Good thing, he thought, the business of plates had gone to the counties in '34. Getting that kind help from Olympia would have taken the kind of time he couldn't spare.

Still, Mac's info had been dead on the money. The car belonged to the Wellington Fish Company, and it turned out Wilhelm Wellington had a grandfather in the Fatherland. Call it a hunch, but adding those facts together only equaled trouble.

As he watched a black sedan drove up to the warehouse. A quick peek through the binoculars told him it was the car he was looking for. Two tall men, both blonde as Carole Lombard, and one with a good six inches on the other that made him look twice as thin as he probably was. Both packed pistols, he could tell by the way their coats bulged at all the wrong spots.

"Hello, sauerkraut," he said.

It bothered him that they were out of uniform, but he couldn't expect Nazis to walk around in their dress threads all the time, especially not when kidnapping was the game of choice they were playing.

The two men met two others near the door, and were ushered inside. Rick knew he needed to get closer.

He saw the door about twenty feet away. Well, he thought, not so much a door as a forgotten corner of a door sneaking one corner out among the boxes piled up against. He considered using it, knowing they'd never expect him to come from behind them, but if it were forgotten on the outside, he could be damn sure it was most likely forgotten and hidden behind boxes inside too.

So much for convenience.

Looks like the front door, he thought. Again. He sighed and inspected his .38 for a full load. He didn't want to need it, but if things turned sour, he'd need his trusted ol' friend at his side.

"Damn!" he said, catching himself and crouching in the shadows again when he saw the broken window. Not big enough to crawl through, but he didn't need to be inside if the sound could make it out to say hello directly to him.

"Looks like I finally caught a break after all," he whispered as he shoved the .38 against his back again.

He creeped to the window, then sidled into the shadows beneath it and listened.

"—don't like it," said one of the guys who had received the two German trees. "It's too risky." An American, born and bred in New York, judging by the accent.

"Be calm, Bernard," said the tallest of the blonde trees. "Chess is best left to the thinkers. Be happy you are a pawn and do your duty."

"Watch your mouth, Kraut."

Clearly, Rick thought, Bernard didn't like being a pawn. But what, he wondered, did that make the trees? Knights? Bishops? Or just taller pawns?

"I still don't like it." Bernard cleared his throat. "That's all I'm saying. He's a lot smarter than we're giving him credit, and that's—"

"He's important only insomuch as he pertains to our plans. And then we don't need him any further."

"Otto?" came a new voice, and Rick assumed it was one of the two receivers.

"Yes, Mr. Killian?"

"Lay off Bernard. He's the best bean counter the Italians can recommend. If he doesn't like the plan, then he doesn't have to."

"Thank you, Mr. Kill—"

"But he still has to do what is expected of him."

There was a long moment of silence.

"Do I make myself clear, Bernard?"

More silence.

"I assure you that my hearing is perfect, but even I cannot hear your brain rattle. When I ask you a question, you will give me an answer, a verbal answer. Do I make myself clear, Bernard?"

"Yes, sir."

"Now," said Killian, "you're certain there will be no trouble with the will?"

"It's iron-clad, sir. You couldn't punch a hole it with a German blade. Trust me."

"Scheiße!" Otto exclaimed. "You've obviously never been at the mercy of a German blade."

"It was an expression, Otto," said Killian. "Calm down. I'm sure Bernard intended no disrespect."

"Yeah, it was what he said, an expression, that's all," said Bernard, his tone clearly not backing up the sentiment.

So Bernie's not a big fan of the Nazis either, Rick thought. It wasn't much, but if push came to shove, and his track record proved it could—and most likely would—he could find a way to use that.

But where, he wondered, was the talk about the politics, about keeping Uncle Oskar from leaving Hitler's master plan and becoming an American? Something didn't add up.

Inside the warehouse a phone rang.

Rick stood up just enough to peek inside the corner of the window. Bernard was a plump, dark-haired man in an ill-fitting suit and desperately in need of a haircut and a shave. Killian, on the other hand, seemed as put-together as if he were one of the Rockefellers. Brown hair. Dark gray suit. Matching fedora. Shoes shiny enough to make out all the way from where Rick was at the window. And a pistol in front of him on the table.

Killian picked up the phone. "Yeah," he said.

Bernard and the trees all focused on Killian.

"It's the boss," he said. "Yeah. What? Who?"

"What?" said the taller tree. Otto.

"Sure thing."

"Inside the warehouse a phone rang."

Killian made a circular motion in the air with his finger then pointed to Otto and the other tree and then at the door.

The Germans nodded and turned around, pulling their pistols from the backs of their slacks.

"Damn," Rick said, pulling the .38 from beneath his coat. "Just my luck."

"Everything smooth on your end, boss?" Killian asked, then waited about fifteen seconds before continuing. "Sure thing. Okay. I'll send the brothers Karamazov as soon as they check things out here."

Rick heard steps around the corner to his right.

"Yeah, yeah, I know it's not Karamazov. It's a joke, okay. Right. Right. Okay. Goodbye."

Well, well, Rick thought, that was that. Nothing more to learn here. Just keep moving right along, sir, thank you very much. He shot a glance to the alley. Only ten or so feet, and he had the darkness to cover him, but there were three problems. One, he'd have to be quiet so he didn't tip off the German around the right corner. Two, the street was in the opposite direction. And three, that meant no access to cabs, and he'd be hoofing in for longer than he had planned. Time was money, sure, but in his business, time could be someone's life too. And time was not his most plentiful resource.

He bit down on his bottom lip. No other choice. The footsteps to the right were growing louder. And now they were joined by footsteps to the left too.

Keeping a tight grip on the .38, he bolted from the window toward the alley.

And slipped on a slimy spot on the pavement.

As he fell he screwed his mouth closed so he didn't yell out.

For all the good it did him.

Instead, before he hit, he tightened his grip on the Colt, and fired a shot down the right side of the back of the warehouse. It split the otherwise silent evening like a cannon's boom.

But that wasn't all.

When he hit the pavement, the impact started at his knee, then the butt of his palm, and the Colt when flying from his grip.

He wiped something thick and wet —which he was sure in the darkness was blood—from his screaming and probably shattered hand, and rolled over to reach for the lost gun. But a gunshot stopped him cold.

"Ve know you are there, Mr. Ruby."

Then silence. Thank God the darkness at least was on his side.

"Ve have been following you and Miss Stein all of the afternoon. It appears you haf ignored our varning from earlier today."

Rick wanted to ask why Otto was putting on such a fake Hollywood German accent when he already knew Otto could speak fluent English. At least he assumed Otto realized he'd been here long enough to hear that much.

But he didn't. Instead, he kept his lips and gums tight and reached through the cutaway pocket in his slacks for the spare Colt holstered around his upper thigh.

You feel good, baby, he thought as his fingers caressed the pistol and pulled it free, through the hole where a pocket should have been.

Another shot cut the air, followed by a shout in German that he couldn't understand. Either Otto's companion didn't know English, or he was keeping the fact that he did close to his chest.

A beam of light found him and lit up his legs.

"Heya, fellas, I found him. He's right here."

The light danced on his chest, and he followed it back to the window where he'd been eavesdropping. The little dark-haired guy, Bernard, stood at the window, shining a flashlight at him, giving the two trees all they needed for a kill shot.

Good thing, he thought with a sigh, the first one missed, flying a foot or so from his head and zinging off the pavement.

He was on his feet in less time than it took him to remember to start breathing again. He hated leaving the .38 behind, but guns were replaceable, even during a slow month. Rick Rubys on the other hand, were one of a kind, and he planned on keeping the one he had around and in jim-dandy shape.

So he ran. Through the alley, then around the office of the Crayton Shipping Co., then through the bar at the mouth of the dock, all the way to 3rd Street on the Southside before he realized the gunshots had faded away.

He sat down against the wall beneath a playbill advertising "Beatrice the Bountiful" doing her strip tease number at the burlesque club across the street.

He waited and caught his breath while the first three cabs passed by.

He waved down the fourth and gave the driver the address for Belle's. Then he politely excused himself for a quick nap during the trip while he heart refused to slow down from the run and instead paved the way for that way-out rhythm that would be waiting for him at the club.

✳ ✳ ✳

Belle noticed him immediately when he walked into the club. So did Evelyn. She even missed a lyric before catching herself and returning to the song, some tune he hadn't heard before, but she never let her eyes leave him. He could feel them even when he sat at the bar and asked Broomstick for a gin and tonic.

"You don't need no gin and tonic," Broomstick told him, and instead handed him a bottle of whiskey.

"You're my best friend, Broomstick," he said. "You know that, right?"

Then Belle walked up behind him, jerked the bottle from his hands and told him to follow her upstairs to his office. "You get this back when I get answers, Rick," she had said.

So he followed them both, Belle and the booze, while Evelyn sang something about a "no-account drunk" and a "cheating heart."

"Rick Ruby, dear sweet heavens above, what's wrong with you, boy?" Belle helped him over to a chair that sat opposite Edie's desk in the front room.

"Thanks, Belle. I love you too," Rick said, slumping into the chair.

"Don't you try to butter me up, boy, not when you insist on coming into my club looking like the bad end of a boxing match. What happened?"

Rick coughed. "I lost a boxing match."

"Rick…" Belle didn't lose her smile, but its tone changed in a way that Rick could recognize instantly. "Don't sass me, boy."

"With the ground. I lost. It won." Rick grinned. "But I plan to demand a rematch next week when I wake up."

Belle pulled Edie's chair opposite him and sat down. She planted her hands on his knees, then locked her eyes on his.

"No more malarkey, Rick. What happened?"

"The new case. I was at the dock checking out a lead, and things turned out bad."

"And?"

"And I fell."

"You fell?"

"I fell hard."

"You fell?"

"Well, there may have been guns involved too."

Belle stood up. "Rick, baby, you worry me so."

"Aw, thanks, Mom, but I'm a big boy now."

"But it ain't me you're gonna have to be worried about. It's Evelyn. She's been on about that woman you left with earlier just about all night. You just better hope you're hurting bad enough to get on her good side again when she finishes."

"Tell her it's just a job."

"Tell her yourself."

"Good idea. Tell me yourself, Rick." Evelyn stood in the doorway, and the hallway light behind her cast her in a silhouette of slender sex that tapered out into a fringed gown. She took a step inside and Rick could swear he heard drums beating out the swagger.

"I'm waiting."

"Hey, Evelyn. You sounded great tonight. What I was able to hear."

Another step. More drums in his head.

"I'm still waiting."

"She's a client."

"You've said that before."

And you've always taken me back, Rick thought, but he knew better than to say it. "And they were."

"But not just clients."

"Come on, baby. There's no need to be—"

"I will be how I damn well want to be, Rick."

"Have I told you lately how beautiful you look when you're angry?"

"Oh, Lord," Belle groaned.

"What?" Rick asked. "It's true."

"Just take your lumps, Rick, so you can take your loving." Belle turned the Evelyn. "You both know as well as I do how and where this night's going to end."

"I don't know if I'm up for—"

"What if you don't have a choice?" Evelyn said.

Rick sighed. "I got shot at tonight, baby."

"You get shot at a lot."

"I think I broke my hand."

"I don't plan to make you use your hand."

"I have a client to check on."

"I have a client you need to check on too."

Another step. More drums. Less Belle. She was walking toward the door, becoming less and less as Evelyn was becoming more and more.

"If you ever want to be with me again, Rick, you will be with me tonight. Show me tonight I'm more important to you than that German singer you went off with."

"You know her?"

The door closed with a click. The room got darker without the hallway light to brighten up the joint. Good ol' Belle, Rick thought.

"We run in the same circles, even though a fair-skinned German wouldn't stoop to compare herself with someone of my color." Evelyn stood in front of Rick. "There are only so many clubs here in New York, and eventually we all get around."

"She's a client."

"She's bad news." Evelyn sat down on Rick's knees. "I've got good news."

"She's a client."

Evelyn wiggled her legs and the slits in the dress fell away to reveal her bare mocha knees pressing up against his thighs. "Want to hear the good news?"

Rick nodded.

"I forgive you for thinking about Gerta that way."

"Listen…"

She leaned in, her face tilted, her lips brushing his own. "I'm listening."

"Really, I've got something important—"

"I know, and I'm right here."

She kissed him, not like courting kisses or friendly kisses, but with something deep and soulful and needy escaping from her open mouth into his own along the curves of her tongue as she wrestled his into submission and he finally returned the passion.

"Mmm. Nice."

"And there's more with that came from."

"Wow."

Evelyn smiled. "Maybe one day we can take that trip to Paris where we might even be able to hold hands and go to a restaurant together in public."

"That would be nice."

"Don't change the subject, Rick."

"Who's changing the subject? I'm up for more of that kissing, and you're talking about vacations."

"Come to my place tonight. Now. With me."

"I…"

"Where is she?"

"At Edie's place." At the mention of Edie's name, Evelyn lips turned down slightly.

"Then she's fine. As tight as she is with God, he wouldn't let nothing happen to them at her place."

"Don't be mean."

"She's sweet on you, Rick."

Rick smiled. "She's a good kid."

"You're a bad man, Rick Ruby." Evelyn shifted forward an inch or so on Rick's lap. "But I just can't stay away from bad men, I guess. You're a weakness of mine, Rick, and you'd better pray I never find the strength to get over it."

Evelyn all but jumped out of his lap when the phone rang.

"Damn," Rick said.

"Don't answer it. Come with me."

"Just let me get this, and then we'll…" He picked up the phone. "Rick Ruby's office. We can find it or shoot it. Your choice. Best rates in town."

Then he grew silent. It was Edie. She was crying.

"I need you here, Rick. I need you. It's…"

"What's wrong, Edie? What's going on, honey?"

"They had guns. I couldn't do anything but watch. Oh God, Rick."

"Who had guns?"

Even Evelyn's expression took on a worried tension at the mention of guns. She stepped forward and put her hand on Rick's shoulder.

"Some Germans."

"Are you okay?"

Edie sniffled more than spoke, but managed to mumble that she was okay.

"And Gerta?"

"They…" Edie coughed and sucked in a loud sniffle. "They kidnapped her."

"They took her?! Damn Nazi bastards!"

"But that's not all, Rick."

"What else, honey?"

"It's Oskar. He's dead."

The death count had begun.

The bucks with badges didn't have to say it. Rick could see it in their stares. Just another Rick Ruby interference with dead bodies raining down to complicate the case.

Rick watched them going over the scene and holding back the crowds already gathering outside Edie's high-rise apartment building. Edie looked at little more than Rick's lapel, her face plastered there as she wept.

"So let's go over this again, Miss Adams. You say two Germans broke in and—"

"No," she said, and Rick felt her face move across his chest as she shook her head. "They were waiting outside."

"I told you to keep them inside, Edie." Rick draped his arm over her shoulder, pulling her closer. Like a kid sister, he told himself, but even he knew it was a lie. In spite of the situation and the dead scientist, he couldn't help but like the way she felt against him. Crazy religious stuff and all, she was still all girl.

"Don't scold me, Rick."

"And why were you heading outside, Miss Adams?"

"I told them we needed to stay in, but the woman, Gerta, insisted on going out for a paper. The old man, Oskar, he went with her to convince her to come back."

"And you?" asked the copper.

"I was with them to keep an eye on them. You see, I promised Rick that I would, and—"

The cop cut him a glare. "Ah, yes. Mr. Ruby. We'll get to him later. Please continue."

"Cut her a break," Rick said, pausing long enough to try to remember the badge's name. But it just wasn't there. "She's told you the story twice already. Can't you see the kid's not in any shape to go through it again?"

Edie looked up slightly. "I'm not a kid, Rick."

I know, Rick thought. Dear God, I know. But he pushed the thought away. Not now. Get a hold of yourself, Rick. Think of Gerta at the mercy of the two Krauts.

The cop only kept his gaze for a few seconds then returned to the notepad in his hand. "So, Miss Adams, after that?"

"They stepped outside and the two Germans—"

"And how did you know they were German?"

"I… Well.. Rick said that…"

"I see. Please continue."

"Wait a minute," Rick interrupted. "She knew they were Germans because I had a run-in with them before and warned her. She must have recognized them from my description."

"Sure, or had the idea planted in her head by your description. You do remember how real police work goes, don't you, Mr. Ruby?"

"I was doing real police work when you were begging your Mama for candy from the five and dime," Rick said, not letting go of Edie. "We're done here."

"We're not done until—"

A thick, meaty hand on the cop's shoulder shut him down.

"We'll contact Miss Adams later if we need further information, Cooper." The man attached to the meaty hand wore a suit that fit like it was made for a larger man, and his dark hair lay mostly hidden beneath a brown fedora. Jack McGinnis, the man who had once agreed to be Rick's best man before Greer's death.

Rick waited for Cooper to make himself scarce.

"Thanks, Mac," he said when Cooper was out of earshot.

"Don't mention it. Young punks think they run the force sometimes." Mac cupped his hands on Edie's shoulders. "You okay, Edie?"

"I'm okay."

"Good girl."

"I didn't mind answering the questions," she mumbled into Rick's chest.

"I know, honey, but I didn't like the way he was badgering you."

"Thanks, Rick."

"Don't mention it. Say, Mac, can you make sure Edie gets home okay?"

Jack nodded. "I'll put a man at the door too."

"You're the best."

"What's on your mind, Rick? Where are you heading?"

"Diner. I was thinking about some of Ernie Biggs's flatcakes."

"Don't give me that. You're going back to the fish place, aren't you?"

"Read me like a book, Mac."

"That's only because you don't go any deeper than third grade, Rick."

"I need answers, and that's the only place I've got left to find 'em."

Mac grabbed Rick's shoulder. "Let me send some men with you."

Rick shook his head. "You know they'd only get in my way."

"Or you'd get in their way."

"Don't you start that noise too."

"I'm serious, Rick. I'm sending some guys."

Rick finally let go of Edie and she looked up at him first, then at Mac, and back to Rick. "Don't let him talk you out of it, Mac."

"Not a chance, Edie."

"At least get her home first. I'll wait if you're serious about cramping my style."

"Saving your life," Edie said.

"Potato, potahto."

"Please, Rick."

"Okay, doll. I'm just going to run by the office for some more ammunition and wait for Mac to call once you're safe at home."

"Promise?"

"On my honor."

"Like that means something," Jack laughed.

"Okay. On Edie's honor then."

"Rick?" she asked.

"Purest thing I could think of, honey."

She smiled. "Find Gerta."

Rick nodded.

He had expected to find the warehouse empty. With the kidnapping and the murder, he was sure Killian, Bernard and the two Germans would have found a new place to hide. He was wrong. Killian and Bernard sat across from each other at a table they had made from a tarp and a crate of fish.

Playing cards.

They stopped when they saw him walk in.

"Where's Gerta?" Rick asked. Once.

His only answer was Killian pushing against the table and knocking over the chair. Bernard grabbed a pistol from the tarp and pointed it at Rick, but Rick was already diving out of the way behind a barrel.

Okay, he thought, once Edie found out he had lied on her honor, she'd be cross, but it wasn't like she hadn't expected it. If she could count on him for anything, it was to know that she couldn't count on him. Not when a case was stuck in his head. And especially not when a dame's life was on the line.

Bernard wasted two shots, neither of which was remotely close to him. One hit the window above him, and the other popped into the pavement a few feet away.

"You'll have to do better than that, Bernard," Rick shouted, just as another shot whizzed a few inches by his right ear. He ducked again behind the barrel.

Apparently Killian had a better aim. Good to know.

"Hey, Killian. I don't know what the game is, but I don't see how killing the old man helps the Nazis at all."

"Don't worry your pretty little head about it, Ruby. All you need to worry about is what color suit do you want your friends to see you in at your funeral."

"If you knew me at all, you'd know that I only wear gray or blue, and my secretary usually picks 'em out for me."

Another shot. This one grazing the side of the barrel.

"Say, Killian, not bad. Think you could give Bernard lessons?"

Bernard wasted another shot in response.

"See what I mean?"

"Laugh it up, Ruby." Bernard this time. "Bet you won't laugh so hard with a hole in your skull."

Rick watched as Bernard stepped into the open. Dumb move, he thought, and he raised the Colt and fired a shot at the idiot's knee. Blood and bone splattered and shattered, and Bernard dropped his pistol and hit the floor howling and crying.

Rick wanted to make a smart-ass comment, but he kept his damn mouth shut this time. Killian was too dangerous an opponent to take chances with now that the comic relief was out of action.

About a minute crawled by without a sound, not even a shot or the shuffle of feet, it seemed.

"So tell me this, Killian. Why would Nazis need a bean counter like Bernard just to keep a scientist loyal to the cause?"

"You're barking up the wrong tree, Ruby, but then again, I always figured you gumshoes were overrated. I blame Hammett and Latimer for stirring up the public and making your type into street legends."

Great, Rick thought. A smart criminal. Those were never as easy as the muscle and the goons. But vanity might be a tact he could use.

"You're too smart to be a crook. You know the bad guy always loses."

"You read too many novels, Ruby."

Rick examined the warehouse. Mostly crates and fish parts. A few boxes and some tool scattered around, but none close enough to be useful.

Fish parts.

It hit him like a bullet in the brain.

Where there's smoke there's fire, and where there's fish guts, there's slippery, dark goo all over the floor, the kind of stuff that would make a dangerous path for someone in a firefight that got moving and didn't stay stuck behind barrels and crates.

Not that the plan didn't come without risk.

Not with Killian being a decent shot and Rick having to be the one to instigate the footfalls.

He took a deep breath, held it, and ran from behind his barrel for the nearest crate.

He waited for the shot, but nothing came.

He peeked above the crate.

No sign of Killian. Nothing moving around the crate he was hiding behind.

Rick let the held breath go finally.

Then took another and ran for the next crate.

Still no shots.

So much for a moving shoot-out. Killian was smarter than he gave him credit.

"Still with me here, Killian?"

The only response came from Bernard, a grunt.

"Radio silence, huh?"

Nothing.

Damn.

Only about ten feet between him and Killian's spot, and not the slightest indication if Killian was still there. For all he knew, Killian could be gone. Or worse, hiding in another spot and getting ready to line up a bullet with the back of Rick's brain.

In for a penny, in for a pound, Rick thought, and left the safety of the crate. Six steps across the concrete. No shots fired. Seven more steps and he all but fell in front of Killian's crate.

He heard it, but not from where he thought Killian was. A trigger clicked, and in the moment of the sound it roared with an echo in the empty warehouse. Rick spun toward the sound like a top.

Bernard.

The idiot was propped on his elbows holding the pistol he'd dropped when Rick shot him. The idiot smiled. Rick could almost see the miniscule movement of his finger.

The cannon-like sound reverberated in the warehouse.

He was dead to rights, and there was no time to move.

I'm sorry, Edie, he felt more than thought. I'm sorry Evelyn. I should have stayed with you tonight. And I'm sorry I couldn't save you, Gerta.

Moments passed, and Rick realized he was still breathing.

Thank God, he thought, that Bernard was a horrible shot.

Bernard targeted him again.

This time Rick was ready.

He twitched his trigger finger on the Colt and blasted Bernard in the face, bringing the death count to two for the case. The cops would have a field day with that. And he'd have to justify lethal force to Mac. But he was alive. And being alive meant he wouldn't have to honor any of those apologies. Yet.

After Bernard lay dead, Rick waited as the warehouse grew quiet again.

Killian either missed his opportunity to get the drop on him or was long gone.

Rick breathed. Once. Twice. A third gasping breath.

Then he settled into the regular rhythm of in and out again.

"Damn," he said. "Damn, damn, damn."

"**R**ick, honey, you need to relax." Belle stood at the bar dealing a game of solitaire. "Broomstick," she said to the tall, skeletal Negro behind the bar. "Get Rick a shot of gin. No. Make it two shots."

"Make it three," Rick said. "It's been a hell of a night."

Evelyn slinked onto the stool beside him. "And one for me too, Bruce."

"It's okay," the tall shadow of a man said. "I like the nickname."

"It's demeaning," she said.

"Does it bother you, Bruce?" Belle asked.

"Nope, ma'am. I like it. It fits me."

"Then it's not demeaning." Belle smiled at Evelyn. "Fight your own battles, baby." She cut her eyes at Rick. "Or you'll lose out."

"Why do I suddenly feel like I'm some kind of prize?" Rick said after downing the first shot of gin. He set the glass on the bar with a loud clink.

"You may be plenty of things, Rick, but one thing you ain't is a prize." Belle smiled.

"Don't I know it, Belle."

"I don't know about that, Rick," Evelyn said, brushing her knee against his thigh.

"Give the boy some room, baby," Belle said. "He killed a man tonight and that never goes down easy."

Rick downed the second shot and placed the second glass with a second clink.

"Got another one of those, Broomstick?"

The bartender nodded and filled both glasses again.

"Thanks."

"Rick?" Evelyn said, no longer touching him.

"Yes, honey?"

"I know I was kinda hard on you earlier, but seriously, are you okay? It scares the hell outta me."

"Didn't do a lot for my nerves either, honey."

"No sign of that other guy?"

Rick shook his head. "I checked. I don't know how he cleaned out without me knowing it, but sure enough, he was long gone." Rick sighed. "Along with my last clue."

"You could always go back to the hotel and make a scene."

"Sure, marching in and knocking around Nazis would be as much fun as anything else I could think of, but my hands are tied. I can't prove they're involved."

"Well, tell Mac what you've seen. He'll believe you. At least he could search for those two tall Germans."

"It's political, baby. Mac's hands are tied too. Unless I have some physical proof…"

"So go back to the warehouse and get photos. Take Mac with you. That'll be proof."

"That warehouse is clean now. They won't be back there."

"Oh."

"It's okay. I know you're trying to help."

"You don't see Rick slipping on sequins and singing, do you, Evelyn?"

Evelyn cut her eyes toward Belle. "What?"

"Then don't try on his suit and his job either."

"Its okay, Belle. It helps me think."

"It's your call, Rick," said Belle.

"Thanks, Rick," said Evelyn.

The phone under the bar clanged, and Rick jumped. Evelyn leaned over quickly and rested one hand on his shoulder and one on his chest. "It's okay, baby. It's just the telephone."

Broomstick reached under the bar and came back up with the split cup handset of the 202. A few years old, but it still worked just fine. "Belle's," he said. "But we closed now."

Rick cocked his head toward Evelyn. "Sorry, honey. I'm a little jumpy."

"Coulda fooled me, baby." She grinned.

Rick smiled.

"Well, you ain't gotta be like that. I'm just telling you that—" Broomstick stopped, his eyes rounding out like huge saucers on his face. "Yes, sir. He's right here."

Everyone was staring at Broomstick now.

He handed the handset toward Rick. "He said he wants to talk to you. It's about that singer, the German woman."

❋ ❋ ❋

Evelyn paced the floor like a jungle cat stalking a meal.

"You should go home," Rick advised. "This is no place for —"

"If you say 'a woman,' Rick, I'm gonna box your ears," Belle intoned from her seat at the bar.

"Yes, ma'am." Rick motioned for Broomstick to pour him another shot of whiskey. "But I was going to say 'you.' I don't think it's safe for Evelyn here."

Evelyn stopped pacing and turned to glare at him. "I'm staying." She locked her hands in place on her wide, curvy hips. "And that's that."

Belle laughed.

"It's dangerous."

"What's dangerous," Evelyn said, "is you putting down that whiskey like the cops are coming to take it away forever. If you're too drunk to keep your head screwed on straight…"

"I do my best thinking when I'm drunk, baby."

"You don't do your best anything when you're drunk, Rick."

"So what's the plan?" Broomstick asked as opened a fresh bottle of whiskey and slid it across the bar to rest beside Rick's two glasses.

Rick took the bottle, tilted it and watched the dark brew drain out until both shots were full again. "There is no plan," Rick said, putting the bottle down. "Something about this just isn't right. They have no reason to come to me. I'm all out of cards. No aces, no kings, not even a damn three in my hand." Rick took a sip. "It smells funny."

"So why agree to the meet up?" Evelyn asked.

"Because I don't have anything, that's why."

"It's a set-up," Broomstick said.

Rick nodded. "Of course it's a set up. But I don't have a choice." He took another sip of the whiskey. "You still got my Sweet Angel behind the bar?"

Broomstick reached beneath the bar, but Rick stopped him. "Don't get her out. Just in case they're watching. Sweet Angel may be the only surprise I have left in this game."

Broomstick grinned.

The door opened.

Everyone shut up and stared at the entrance.

The shorter of the two Germans Rick had seen earlier stood highlighted by the midnight glow of lights from down the avenue. He wore dark trousers and a brown sweater and matching cap. A gun-shaped bulge at his side under the bottom of the sweater at the waist of his trousers told Rick he wasn't fooling around. He stepped inside but said nothing. Instead he examined the room, his eyes lingering on doors and the edges of chairs and tables, anywhere someone might be hiding for an ambush.

"Hello," Rick said. "Welcome to Belle's." He tapped out a cigarette and lit it. Belle glared at him. He put it out.

The German still refused to speak. Instead he walked further inside and went directly to the door opposite the bar, opened it and disappeared into the hallway for a few moments. Rick waited, and soon he returned, shutting and locking the door behind him. Then he did the same at the door beside the bar, leading to the storeroom. After that, the giant Nazi started to kick up rugs and check under them for panels in the floor.

"If you want to meet, that's fine, but if you just want to come in and trash my joint, I'd really rather you not."

The German stopped, glared at Belle, then looked away again as if she weren't worth his time or effort.

"There's a panel to the cellar," she said, "but it's in the hallway, out there where you locked it. The last thing I need is people accidently falling through my floor in here while they're dancing."

The man ignored her and kept searching. Rick watched him work and downed the remainder of the first shot glass, followed quickly by the contents of the second glass.

After nearly two minutes more of silent searching, the German left the bar and let the doors clink shut behind him.

Rick looked at Belle. Belle looked back at him. Evelyn stopped pacing and stood behind Rick, her head at his right shoulder and arm around his left.

"Is it just me, or does anybody else think that was strange?" she asked.

"Just doing his work, baby."

"Just messing up my floor is more like it," Belle said.

Rick forced a smile.

"I'd feel a lot better if you weren't here, honey," Rick whispered to Evelyn.

"If I left now, after tall, white and blonde just did all that work, I'm sure it wouldn't be appreciated."

"I suppose." Rick felt her hand tighter on his shoulder. "But I can't help feeling like it's a bad idea, you being here."

She rose up on her tip-toes and whispered directly into his ear, her

"The doors opened again and the German re-entered the club"

breath raising the tiny hairs on his ear. "I've been taking care of myself long before I met you, Rick Ruby. Don't you worry none. I can handle myself in all kinds of trouble." She took a seat at the bar beside him.

The doors opened again and the German re-entered the club. Only he wasn't alone this time. Behind him was Killian, in a navy blue double-breasted suit with the gray fedora from the warehouse. The next to enter was another German, the tallest of the two trees, in a brown suit. He held tightly onto Gerta's arm and pushed her inside over the threshold as much as guided her. She clutched her black purse like a vise.

"Gerta?" Rick asked when he saw her.

"I'm okay, Rick. They don't want to ki—"

The German spun her around to face him then slapped her hard on the jaw. "No talking. The next one could ruin your singing voice, so I'd advise you to remember the rules."

"Take it easy, Otto," Rick said, enjoying the look of surprise that lit up the Nazi's face. "I'm a good listener. I know more than you think," Rick added. Maybe I can bluff a straight even without cards, he thought.

Otto took Gerta to a table in the middle of the room, and pushed her into a chair. Then he sat down beside her without easing his grip on her arm. Killian tipped his hat at Rick, then took a seat beside Otto. The tallest German stood by the door, his hand at his side, near the pistol at his waist.

"I admit I'm curious why you'd call, Otto. And I'm even more curious where you're boss is, the one who called and turned you and Silent Treatment over there loose on me at the warehouse."

Otto didn't answer.

"Don't like it," Killian said. "Too many people here."

"Too many people Mr. Ruby cares about," Otto said. "It will keep him…" He turned and caught Rick's eyes, then smiled as he said, "compliant."

Rick felt the lump in his throat and took a deep breath to swallow it.

"I want music," Otto said, turning to Belle. "Tell the Negro harlot I want her to sing."

Evelyn would have gotten up off her stool and made the situation worse, no doubt, if Rick hadn't gripped her thigh hard enough to make her wince. She looked at him and he shook his head. "Just play along."

"I'm not a harlot, and I will not have anyone—"

"Save it for the right time, honey." Rick loosened his grip. "Please."

"The band's gone home," Evelyn stated the obvious.

"The skinny one at the bar, do you play?" Otto asked. "Don't all of your kind play jazz?"

Rick's hand latched onto Evelyn's leg again.

"No, sir," Broomstick said. "I guess I'm part German."

The German at the door pulled his pistol and trained it on Broomstick.

"Mr. Ruby?"

"Yeah, Otto?"

"Tell your Negro to apologize before my brother shoots him."

"Broomstick?" Rick said, then added. "But he's not my anything other than my bartender. Pours a hell of a Scotch too. Would you like one?"

"Sorry, sir," Broomstick said, his grin threatening to get him shot in the face anyway.

"Can't sing without music," Evelyn said smugly.

"Oh hell," Killian said, pushing his chair away from the table and standing. "Do you know 'The Varsity Drag'?"

Evelyn nodded.

"It's a happy song, I trust," Otto said. "I never liked the blues. Not appropriate for..." He stroked his barren chin. "...Germans."

"I'll just bet," Evelyn said.

"Cool it, honey. Don't pull the trigger yourself."

"I'm not doing this for you, Otto," she said as she rose from the stool and followed Killian to the stage. The gangster sat at the piano, cracked his knuckles and began to play.

"Damn," Rick said. "He's good. Didn't expect that."

Killian lit up. "Thank ya, Rick. There's more to life than shooting and stealing, sometimes. Even a man like me needs a hobby."

Evelyn picked up the rhythm and bit into it with her usual gusto. "We've always thought knowledge is naught, we should be taught to dance," she sang. In spite of herself, it looked to Rick, she let the music seep into her and with Killian banging away on the piano, who would just as soon shoot her in the back as well as back her up as a pianist, she started to sway and all but make love to the melody. For nearly a minute and a half, no one said a word. They just watched as Evelyn commanded their attention.

That's my girl, Rick thought, and he knew he had to make sure she survived the night. For his sake as much as any other reason.

It was Otto who broke the silence. "Very nice," was all he said.

"A round of the good stuff, Broomstick," Belle said.

Otto shook his head. "A beer. German beer. And one for my brother."

The man at the door shook his head.

"And for you, Miss Gerta?" Belle asked.

"Give her nothing."

"You're the man with the gun, honey," Belle said.

"Have Mr. Ruby bring it to me. You and the other…" He clearly was fighting his natural choice of words. "…person stay at the bar."

Rick took a deep breath and grabbed the drink, winked at Belle, whispered "Trust me," and carried the beer and his own fresh shot of liquor to the table where Otto and Gerta sat.

"Hello, doll," he said as he sat opposite the German-born singer. A little worse for wear, but her legs and make-up were still doing their job, as far as he was concerned. But those eyes of hers, they had lost their dark fire. She hadn't had it easy.

"How are you holding up?"

She looked at Otto, waiting for his permission to speak, Rick guessed. Otto nodded.

"I'm okay, Rick, but my uncle…" She fell to the table, sobbing.

"Plenty of time for the waterworks later, honey. Let's just see what Otto wants first." Rick popped his neck and gave Otto his full attention. "So, as I see it, you want to buy my silence about everything I saw at the warehouse in exchange for Miss Stein's safety."

Otto smirked.

"Or I could be wrong," Rick said, smiling. "It's rare, but it's been known to happen occasionally."

"A joker until the end, I see."

"A man can die with a smile or a grimace."

Gerta sobbed quietly opposite him.

The music stopped, then Killian started to play something equally bouncy.

Evelyn began to croon again. "I've got the world on a string, sitting on a rainbow…" As she sang she stepped from the stage and began her act in earnest, just like it the club was full of drunks and other customers. She walked toward them with her hips swinging like jungle drums, and walked past them to continue slink around the club from empty table to empty table.

Even the German at the door started to watch her, Rick noticed.

I'll be damned, he thought. He looked at the bar. Broomstick had one hand on the bar and the other beneath it, presumably on Sweet Angel. Belle had her eyes closed, praying to the Good Lord that Evelyn knew what she was doing, he thought.

"Otto?" Rick asked.

"What?"

Rick scanned the room. The tree at the door had his eyes on Evelyn's jungle drums as they traced sex among the tables.

"I'd be a silly so-and-so if I should ever let you go," she sang, cocking her elegant profile over her shoulder to bat her eyes at the tree, and Rick knew it was now or never.

He stomped Gerta's foot under the table, and when she cried out and jerked up, Otto turned to see what happened. When he did, Rick flipped the table against Otto, pushing Gerta away to his side.

The tree at the door pointed his pistol at Rick, but it was too late. Broomstick had both barrels of Sweet Angel locked onto him. One blow from the hand-cannon sent the man down in a crumbled lump of Aryan flesh.

The music stopped and Killian reached at his back for his own firearm, but Rick swung wide with one of his .38s and Killian thought better of the idea and dropped his arms at his side. Otto lay under the table, with Rick's weight pushing it down on him and locking his arms crossed on his chest, unable to draw his own weapon.

"Looks like the tables have turned, Nazi."

Otto grunted beneath the weight of both Rick and the table.

"Stay still, because I don't have a single reason not to blow a hole in your face. Understand me?"

"I think you have a very good reason not to do that, Rick."

He jerked to the side where Gerta's voice pulled him. She stood with her arm locked around Evelyn's neck. His missing .38 gripped in her hand and pointing at Evelyn's temple. Her purse lay discarded in the floor. "Oh hell."

"Yes." Gerta grinned and called out to Killian. "Come out from behind the piano, you coward."

He did.

"Take Rick's gun."

Rick handed his new .38 to Killian.

"And I wouldn't reload the shotgun, Mr. Broomstick," Gerta said. "At least not if you like seeing this whore in one piece."

"Put it down, Bruce," Rick said. "It's not worth Evelyn's life."

"What the hell is going on here?" Belle yelled. "We were trying to save your life, girl."

Gerta grinned. "And while I do appreciate the effort, I really do, it wouldn't help me get what I'm looking for."

"She was never in any danger," Rick said. "Damn it. How could I have missed it? It was a set-up from the beginning."

"Distracting you is easy as pie, my dear. A flash of leg. A kiss. A little jealousy to stir up the other women in your life and keep you unfocused."

"Rick…" Evelyn choked out the words through the grip Gerta had on her thin neck.

"Ssshh, girl. I'm talking." Gerta turned to Rick, who was helping Otto to his feet. "You see, Rick, the best lies are based on truth. My uncle really was truly looking to leave the Nazis and come to the United States. But because of his importance to the Reich, Uncle Oskar was worth a great deal of money, money that would come to his only surviving heirs when he died."

Rick laughed. "And if he left Germany's favor, he'd have forfeited all the dough."

"So you see why we couldn't let that happen."

Gerta pushed Evelyn to Otto. "Watch her, but not like Hans did."

"Her kind does not interest me, Gerta."

"I like to think that I—" Evelyn started, but stopped when Otto's arm cut off her breath.

"I told you to hush, whore," Gerta said. "Now, where were we, Rick?" Gerta motioned for him to sit in the chair even though the table was no longer there.

"It all makes sense. You needed a patsy. That's the only reason your 'kidnappers' would have had to contact me out of the blue."

Gerta smiled. "You are a very handsome man, Rick Ruby, but you're not particularly smart." She knelt beside him and let her words ride her breath into his ear. He shuddered. "If only you hadn't left me with your secretary, you could have gotten something out of the arrangement too." She closed the already tiny gap between her lips and his ear. "We both could have."

"I guess I'll have to live with the disappointment."

She stood up. "Fortunately for you, darling. You won't have to live with the disappointment long." As she walked away, she traced a line from his waist down the top of this thigh all the way to his kneecap.

"Let's move this show along, can we?" Killian chimed in. "I'd like to be able to spend my share before I'm too old to enjoy it."

"Very well, Mr. Killian. Please hand me Rick's gun."

He did.

"The matching set," she said. "It's such a shame."

"What's that, doll?" Rick asked.

She raised the .38. "That Mr. Killian was tragically killed in the firefight."

Rick saw the flush rise in Killian's face when he realized he'd been played for a patsy too. And that he had just given his own murderer the weapon she would use to kill him.

He tried to turn toward the door, but it was too late. One .38 caliber bullet entered above his eye and exited the other side of his head, just behind his ear. Blood and brains exited with the bullet, and Killian's soulless corpse fell to the ground on buckled knees.

"You were very fortunate to manage to kill one of your assailants, darling." Gerta traced Rick's jawline with the barrel of the pistol.

"Just let them go. You can kill me, but they've got nothing to do with it."

"Don't be stupid, Rick. Witnesses."

"At least make it painless. For me. Please."

Gerta scrunched up her eyes in thought. "Perhaps," she said. "Except for your whore."

Rick saw the rage in Evelyn's eyes even though her voice was cut short by Otto's arm.

"I don't like the way she looked at me earlier. She genuinely loves you, darling, but she's also smart enough to know she can't have you to herself."

"Just make it painless, please."

"Not for her."

"Please."

"She has lived her whole live in pain, Rick. Why should that change now?"

Rick locked his eyes onto Evelyn's. He was so focused that it took another gunshot to draw him away.

"Bruce!"

It was Belle. Broomstick was nowhere to be seen.

"She killed Bruce! The—"

I'd choose your next words carefully, Belle," Gerta said. "But first…" She raised the .38. "Move the girl, Otto, unless you want to share her bullet."

"Yes, Gerta."

"Good boy."

Evelyn squinched her eyes tightly. Rick kept his on Gerta, looking for the extra seconds he needed to get out of the damn chair and stop her from killing the woman he… loved? Did he love anyone but himself? Could he? Regardless, she deserved better than this. Better than him, for damn sure.

His shoes pushed against the floor as he watched Gerta's finger pull the trigger of his own damn gun. The boom thundered in his ears, followed by Belle's scream. He collapsed, his knees suddenly as weak as milk.

The room fell quiet.

"What?" came the surprising sound of Evelyn's voice.

Rick lurched up, but the .38 spun around in Gerta's hand and stopped at his forehead.

"Sit down, darling. The show is still going."

Rick took in the sight of Evelyn standing, her eyes wide and dark, her skin as pale as he'd ever seen it. But alive. Somehow wonderfully alive.

"Do you think I wasn't going to save this whore for last, Rick? I want you to see everyone else go first. Then her. Then and only then will it be your turn, darling."

Rick examined the room. A dead lump of brown tweed lay beside the spot where Evelyn was riveted to the floor. Otto.

"Why share the wealth?" Rick asked with more inflection that he had intended.

Gerta nodded. "Family is overrated."

Rick had seen enough. There was only Gerta and the gun left. It was the best opportunity he was going to get, and he knew it. He dove from the chair for the murderous singer, but she moved like lightning and put two shots through his shin, and he screeched and hit the floor, blood thickening the dark material of his trousers.

"I'm sorry, Evelyn," he said.

"Tell Broomstick hello," Gerta said and pointed the pistol at Belle. The older woman didn't cry or beg and even change her expression. All she did was take one step closer.

"Damn it," Rick grunted, trying to put weight on his knee.

"Ugh."

A weak sound. Behind the bar. Broomstick. In pain, but still alive. Just how alive, Rick had no idea. Belle's face relaxed.

"What?" Gerta scowled. "Still alive?"

Rick grabbed the chair beside him and pressed his weight against it to pull himself to his knees.

Gerta walked to the bar.

"Hello, Broomstick," Belle said.

Gerta swung the pistol, catching Belle in the jaw, and the older woman went down. "Just wait. Your turn is coming."

Rick looked at Evelyn. The color was returning to her face. Her breathing was deepening, but she was still in shock.

"Broomstick!"

"Rick?"

Rick saw the twin barrels of Sweet Angel peek over the top of the bar and stop Gerta cold.

Rick stood up, grimacing, but doing his best to ignore the hell that was burning in his leg.

"Shoot her!" Belle yelled.

Rick grabbed the chair that had helped him up.

Sweet Angel's trigger clicked.

Gerta's breathing locked up.

But only for a moment.

The barrel was empty. Sweet Angel wasn't ready to sing.

Gerta's own finger twitched on the .38.

Rick's breathing stopped.

But the .38 said nothing either.

"Gerta," Rick said weakly.

She turned.

"You should have put the bullets in my head," he said and swung the chair like a caveman's club.

The legs connected with her face and dug tracks of dirt and blood across her pale skin. She stood for a mere moment—just long enough for him to see the dark eyes roll go dim and roll back—before she flew back and crashed into the bar.

Rick swung what was left of the chair and hit her on the other side of her face. This time she fell away from the bar and crumpled into the floor beside Belle.

Rick raised the remaining leg for another strike, but two mocha hands slithered over his shoulders and rested on his chest. Warmth pushed against his back. He felt his breathing return.

"It's over, baby."

The curve of a familiar cheek rested against his shoulder.

"She's out cold."

"Evelyn," he said. Not asked. "Is Broomstick…"

Belle answered. "He's in better shape than you, Rick. The bullet just grazed his arm."

"Lucky me," Rick said.

"Baby," Evelyn said, her hands leaving his chest and her warmth slinking around his side until she rested under his arm and supported his weight. "Let go. I've got you."

And he did. His knee buckled beneath him and he dropped. Evelyn caught him but the effort it took her was evident on the lines of her face.

"Call the cops."

"Belle's already doin' it."

His eyes felt black. Like the pain in his leg. "It's bad, ain't it?"

"You gonna need new suit pants, that's for sure."

"I'm sorry."

"You rest now, baby."

And he did.

"Hey, baby."

Rick felt the kiss push his lips apart but didn't see it. He refused to open his eyes.

"How's the leg?"

"Hurts like hell."

"I bet."

Another kiss.

Eyes still closed.

"What day is it?"

"Sunday. Wanna sleep in?"

"Well, except for maybe the sleeping."

"You're a bad man, Rick Ruby."

"Yeah, I know. It's a good thing you ain't strong enough yet to get over me."

"You're cute when you're right, baby."

He felt a leg slip between his own. Bare. Not a trace of silk anywhere.

"Evelyn?"

"Yeah, baby?"

"Where's your nightgown?"

"On the dresser."

"And where's your leg?"

"You know damn well where my leg is."

"Thought so."

Another kiss. This one leaving his lips parted just slightly.

"You gonna open your eyes this morning?"

"Depends."

"On what?"

"What time is it?"

Evelyn moved, and he felt her weight shift on top of him.

"Seven a.m."

"In that case, no." He grinned. "It's too damn early to open my eyes."

"Your loss, baby."

He felt Evelyn push her chest against his own. He opened his eyes.

Her face came into focus above his. Her lips gently caressing the tip of his nose. Her eyes smiling at his bleary eyes. Her hair brushed back straight and long so that it cascaded from the side of her face onto his face.

"Be careful."

"Ain't I always?"

"No."

She smiled. "I thought you liked dangerous women, Rick Ruby."

"Evelyn?" he asked. "Is this…"

Judging from her eyes, she didn't like the serious tone in his question.

Her knee shifted up. Her toes tickled his good knee. He shut up.

"How 'bout another one of those kisses?" he asked. "I like those."

She smiled. "I'm glad."

"You're one hell of a nurse."

"I'm an awful nurse." She pressed her lips against his. "Would a good nurse do this?" she asked after the kiss.

"Not many of them."

She pushed up and smacked his chest. "Rick Ruby!"

"C'mere." He wrapped his hands around her shoulders and pulled her down again.

"Mmm," she mumbled.

The phone rang.

She broke the kiss.

"Let it ring," he said.

"It might be news about Bruce."

"It'll keep."

She smiled, then rose from the bed and got the phone.

"Hello," she said. Then, "Yeah, he's here. Hold on."

She pulled the phone as far as it would reach. Rick met her at the edge of the bed. "Who calls this time of morning?"

Evelyn scowled. "Your secretary."

"Oh. I'll make it quick." He spoke to the receiver. "It's Rick, honey."

"Good morning, Rick," Edie said. "And you will not make this quick. You'll do no such thing."

"What's the noise, honey?"

"I was just calling to tell you that Carla's back in town. Remember her? Remember her daddy who hates your guts?"

"Oh."

"Well, she read about your incident in the paper and came all the way back here from Washington to, and I quote, 'nurse you back to health.'"

"Oh."

"She's meeting you at your place after lunch."

"Good, that gives me—"

"That gives you no time at all. I need you to be ready and waiting for me with your crutches in hand in twenty minutes."

"I don't get it, baby."

"Oh, no, Rick. You will not get out of your promise that easily this time, hurt leg or not."

"Oh damn."

"Language, Rick. We're going to God's house."

"The mission. I forgot."

"That's why I reminded you."

"Good ol' Edie."

He was sure he could hear her smile through the phone.

"And Rick?"

"Yeah, Edie?"

"I forgive you."

"For forgetting?"

"Not only that."

"What's she saying?" Evelyn asked, her arms slinking around his waist.

"Yeah, okay, whatever. I'll be ready." Rick tossed the receiver toward the cradle and missed. It hit the floor with a clank.

"Well?"

"What are you doing later tonight, honey?"

"Rick."

"Sorry, honey. I've got to get ready for church." Rick stood up, felt the pain in his knee, and reached for his crutches. "Damn."

Evelyn watched without smiling.

"You're a bad man, Rick Ruby, an awful bad man."

"I know, baby. I know. But even I'm not bad enough to break a date with God."

Rick knew he'd be okay when he saw the corners of Evelyn's mouth turn up. He returned the smile.

"I've got a few minutes to spare though," he said.

"Oh, no," Evelyn said. "I'm going with you." She smiled and went into the bathroom.

Rick let go of the crutch and fell back onto her bed.

"Oh boy. I should've tried harder to get killed."

"Like I'd let you get off that easy."

The End

My Heroes Haven't Always Been Cowboys
(or, God Bless You, Mr. Bogart)

There's an old country song that says, "My heroes have always been cowboys," and for kids growing up in the generation prior to mine, that was most likely true. But for me, as a kid, my heroes came from two other places than out West—comic books and Star Wars.

Brightly costumed people who could move planets or shoot lasers from their eyes. Valiant space samurai with laser swords and wise-cracking robot comic relief. The stuff a young boy's dreams are made of.

Then I grew up. And found the stuff a—ahem—maturing boy's dreams are made of.

(But let me back up a second. Even as I grew up, I never completely turned my back on comic books heroes in tights and Star Wars heroes. But I added some more grown up heroes to their ranks.)

Enter Humphrey Bogart.

I still remember with gusto the first time I saw Bogey as Raymond Chandler's Philip Marlowe in *The Big Sleep* and as Dashiell Hammett's Sam Spade in *The Maltese Falcon*. Just one cocky line to the coppers, one snarky come-on to the femme fatale, one left hook to a crook's glass jaw, and I knew I was hooked. (I learned how to whistle too, for the record, thanks to Bogey's costar, but that's another tale for the telling.) The addiction only grew stronger when I discovered Stacey Keach as Mike Hammer (in both TV versions, thank you very much), and later, the old radio show and television show featuring Richard Diamond.

There was something about these renegade men that appealed to the kid in me who needed someone not only to root for but to try to emulate. Sure, we all knew that smoking was bad for you and that you shouldn't treat a lady like sexual property, but when the private dicks did it, it seemed somehow... innocent... as if a mere throwback to an era when it was all okay and kind of, well, expected.

Of course, looking back, I know now it was pure fantasy.

In reality, private detectives seldom got the girl, more often than not got stuck photographing cheating lovers, and rarely got to beat the cops out of any famous murder cases. And they never, ever, ever had leggy dames with curves like the coast of Florida lining up outside their offices for double entendres, sultry seductions and hard-boiled adventures.

But honestly, none of that mattered.

Because, just like comic book super heroes and Star Wars space adventurers, they were all too real when I opened a book or turned on the TV or popped in a DVD (or a video cassette at the time—screw you, I'm old).

This story grew from that fake realness. I knew where it had to begin and where it had to end. At Belle's. The bar. The club. The dive. Or as Rick knows it… home.

I knew that just like I knew Rick had to be caught up in the grip of all the women he thought he could manipulate. And I knew that hubris would be the kryptonite to ensnare him and almost get him killed.

Time and time again.

But for now, for this story, it all began with a single image, a black and white photograph in my brain: a leggy singer in a smoky bar, an alluring client at a table, and one exasperated P.I. stuck between them, both literally and figuratively.

Just like it should.

So thanks to this volume of tales, the pulp P.I. lives on. The femme fatale lives on. The good girls who hit as hard and drink as much as the bad girls live on. The glass-jawed crooks live on. The double entendres live on. Even the sexist jerk with the heart of gold lives on, albeit tempered a bit (but not too much, let's hope and pray) through the eyes of his contemporary re-creators.

Together with Bobby Nash, I helped to create Rick Ruby from the memories of Mike Hammer, Richard Diamond, Phillip Marlow, and the other great pulp detectives of the '30s, '40s and '50s. I don't expect that we'll see his name in the line-up of the great detectives one day alongside his inspirations, but damn if that wouldn't be some awesome icing on the P.I. cake.

For now, I'm just thrilled to know that you were intrigued enough to give ol' Rick a shot and pick up this first volume of his adventures. I say first because, trust me, there will be more as long as talented writers are eager to write them. And me too. Because now that Rick and Edie and Evelyn and Carla and Mac and Belle and Broomstick have gotten themselves wormed into my brain, I don't expect them to let me go free any time soon.

There are lots of great new memories to be made here. And I'm sure Rick is tickled, well, any color other than pink, to be a part of 'em.

SEAN TAYLOR writes prose, graphic novels and comic books (yes, Virginia, there is a difference between comic books and graphic novels). In his writing life, he has directed the "lives" of zombies, super heroes, goddesses, dominatrices, bad girls, pulp heroes, and yes, even frogs.

He's the former managing editor of Campfire (formerly Elfin) graphic novels. He's also been a staff writer, managing editor and editorial vice president for iHero Entertainment's *Writer's Digest* Grand Prize Zine Award-winning *Cyber Age Adventures* magazine ("The very first zine award, as a matter of fact," he adds with great pride).

He's also the former editor-in-chief of Shooting Star Comics, and he has written and edited for the role-playing game industry, having contributed to the *DCU Role Playing Game* published by West End Games. He's the former editor for the Baptist Men Edition of *On Mission* magazine and the former associate editor of *On Mission* magazine. He has won several awards for his periodical and fiction work and has contributed articles and book and music reviews to many national periodicals.

For more information visit www.taylorverse.com.

RUBIES & DIAMONDS

The Birth of Rick Ruby

(In which The Ruby Files co-creators go behind the scenes and confess all their dirty little secrets)

By Sean Taylor and Bobby Nash

Sean: Okay. Just so you don't have to think about it too hard or too long, yes, there is a strong similarity between the names Rick Ruby and Richard Diamond. Can we just get that out of the way first? Why? Because Diamond paved the way, as it were, for Rick Ruby to be born.

Time for the backstory.

Several years ago, I got this crazy idea to approach a pulp publisher about launching an all-new, all-prose series of adventures featuring the late, great gumshoe Richard Diamond. It was shortly after I had picked up a cheap DVD set of detective TV shows and had fallen off my gourd, infatuated with the pulp styling of the 1950s *Richard Diamond* show that starred David Jannsen in the title role.

Bobby: So, several years ago, Sean comes to me with this crazy idea. Okay, so maybe it wasn't all that crazy because I liked the idea of doing a pulpy detective series. By this time I'd only flirted with crime pulps on a Domino Lady story. It was fun and I wanted to rejoin the pulpy noir-ish world of the private detective. As usually happens when a new project starts to take shape, I was ready to dive in and start writing.

And then we hit a snag.

Sean: Well, as often happens in this business, you discover the obstacles in the road to your dreams. First, it was becoming very confusing to discover (without dropping major bucks to a real copyright lawyer) if Richard Diamond the character was as public domain as Richard Diamond the specific episodes. Sure, there were plenty of TV shows and radio dramas in the public domain with Richard in them, but Richard himself wasn't as clearly delineated as "up for free."

Bobby: There's nothing so loud as the sound of a dream project shattering into thousands of tiny little pieces, but such is the nature of the creative beast.

Sean: However, that didn't make the hankering to write his hard-boiled tales wane in the least, which left Bobby and me with three options:

Fork out a wad of cash to take a chance people who read books might actually remember Richard Diamond and buy his books IF he was indeed public domain (hence needing the wad of cash to learn).

Just chuck the idea and go on about our merry way with the handful of other projects we were both already involved in.

Take the kernel and the basic idea, reshuffle the specifics and cast, and roll out something brand new that felt familiar.

Thankfully, we chose option three, and Airship 27 Productions was there to support us.

Bobby: Well, since neither Sean nor Bobby has (or had) a wad of cash to fork out (we are freelance writers after all, and despite popular misconceptions, rich we are not), and we really hated to walk away from the idea, we started exploring other options.

That's where The Pulp Factory comes in. The Pulp Factory is a Yahoo Group of New Pulp writers, artists, editors, publishers, and other creative folk. We have some mighty fine discussions and one day that discussion turned to classic hardboiled pulp private detectives and how cool it would be to see some New Pulp writers take a crack at it.

Sean mentioned our aborted Richard Diamond idea, which was well received. Long story short, Airship 27 Chief Ron Fortier liked the idea and asked if Sean and I would be interested in spearheading the project to get it off the ground.

Sean and I got together over a steak dinner (rather apropos, I thought) and we started nailing down Rick's world and supporting cast. One of the fun things I'll always remember from that evening was how the people at the surrounding tables were trying to look as though they weren't eavesdropping on our rather spirited, and interesting, conversation about guns, booze, jazz, dives, and women. Oh, the women.

Sean: Of course, the similarities to Richard Diamond now stop at the name. There's just way too much of all the other famous and some not so famous gumshoes in his personality and that of his regular cast. You can't read Rick's exploits without seeing shades of Philip Marlowe or Sam Spade. You can't help but see the poorly worn suit. You can't help but see all the roles ever played by Lauren Bacall and Veronica Lake as you read about the ladies who wander in and out of Rick's life and adventures. You can't help but see the influence of the 1930s pulps, the 1940 film noir movies, the 1950s detective shows, and the throwbacks to that genre during the television of the 1970s and all the way up to today too. Brass knuckles and bombshells. Swinging hips and swanky dives. Deadly guns and dark adventures.

And you can't discount the imaginations of not just Bobby and me, but also Andrew and William for adding to Rick's mythos and (what the kids call nowadays) swagger.

Bobby: As much fun as Sean and I had creating this world that Rick Ruby inhabits, I think the other writers really brought an added dimension. Rick is an enigma. He's part Sam Spade, part Jim Rockford, part Magnum P.I. Rick has swagger and smarts, but doesn't always make the right decisions. Rick likes to drink a little too much and has never met a lady he couldn't love if she'd just let him. He's a 1930s man's man, and we're loving every minute of living in his world.

Sean: More than anything, I'll just thrilled to know that the great pulp P.I. lives on and that I'm able to be part of a new generation of writers still influenced by the character archetype and able to hopefully continue the tradition and influence others to eventually do the same. Long live Rick Ruby. (No matter how often he insists on trying to get himself killed.)

Bobby: Agreed. I hope this is just the beginning of many Ruby Files we crack open. We're already prepping a second volume of stories, and I suspect a volume three will follow suit. We're happy you decided to join us for the ride.

Now go find yourself a seat. The show's about to start and Evelyn hates it when you talk during her set.

We'll talk more in volume two.

Bobby Nash and Sean Taylor
Hanging out at Belle's